Last Exit
to Balham

Angie Alderman

Last Exit to Balham

© Angie Alderman 2018

All rights reserved.

ISBN-13: 978-1722210595

First Printing: 2018

Foreword

When Zoe Sender gets ploughed down by a speed freak cyclist, she has no idea that she is about to embark on an identity crisis.

She has no idea how to help herself.

All she knows is with only one hundred days until her significant birthday, she must find a way to fathom out the big things in life.

To find her way back home.

Acknowledgements

To my parents, *Margaret and Allen Alderman* for their love and support in everything I do; and to *Michael Wylie* for being my first reader.

I sincerely hope you enjoy reading this story, as much as I enjoyed living it.

Dedication

For Everyone Who's Left.

Contents

Last Exit to Balham

Little Earthquake

Little Piggy,

Busy Street,

Motor Car,

Sausage Meat

(Mum 1978)

Bouf, just like that, everyone was leaving. Going…going…gone. Creeping up on you when you least expected it, like a bolt of lightning lacerating the earth on a hot summer's day. You find your stomach is in convulsions and someone is standing in front of you waving good-bye. As a wailing mourner all you can do is to remind yourself that like all moments, this will pass. After all it's not that bad. The familiarity does eventually become reassuring.

'It's not you, it's me…'

'The timing isn't right, see ya…'

What is the aversion of staying together? Are we trying to avenge our parents who forcibly turn us into school at the tender age of four and a half tiny years, when we have already done time, months old in creches, other people's homes, and with relatives we don't like? Dumped and left behind. Is this the first scar of abandonment etched into our nervous system? Is it from here that our flight begins? Plucked from the warm embrace of our parental world to be thrust into a dank room reeking of sour milk, urine, and crayons. Is it from here we are on the run? Doomed as adults to accumulate farewells as part of an innate sense of survival as it is, after all, what we know. The friend, the lover, the cousin, the dog - they all leave.

It was Thursday night in London. I felt divided; on one hand compassionate, bright, breezy, happy, and all those things that suggest a perfect state of mind. At the same time there was this nagging feeling of despair as if someone had just covered the Norwegian Christmas tree in Trafalgar Square, with black plastic and spoilt the fun. I scanned the papers, surfed the net, and went in search of something to make me feel better. Holistic weekends were populating in the search menu in volumes. Everything from mindfulness, mediation courses, yoga, gong therapy, aroma, light. You could learn how to do the Runes, Feng shui your home, or get an astrology chart completed. The selection was endless. Did I now need to consult the I Ching to see which option to take? Should I take a course of acupuncture to help with my decision making? With so many choices, given it was the end of the week, a *Life Course* did seem like the most suitable thing to do, after all – it would only take two days. I could be sorted by Monday.

Dexter, my bedsit - next door - sort of roommate, flat share and friend, agreed to feed Taxi the cat. A beautiful black and white fluffy tailed creature who looked like a spider monkey. Perhaps she was a spider monkey in a past life? Anyway, I knew this was going to be the best forty-eight hours of my life. The course guaranteed a clarity, and perspective; a colonic irrigation of the mind. I quickly registered, and then downloaded the one sheet pre-requisite to registering and headed towards Balham tube.

Blimey, there were so many rules: No smoking, no caffeine, no chocolate, no alcohol, no drugs, no chewing gum, no swearing, no lateness. I was already late, looking for decent underwear. If I was going to an intense workshop about the self, I needed to feel the best I could, so I prepared for the event with the same attention as going on a date. Since I hadn't managed to get to the launderette (washing machine was still broken, it wasn't under warranty anymore and too old to have fixed) it had to be the all-in-one swim suit under a baby doll dress. Nan had previously suggested because of travelling a lot I should invest in paper knickers in case of emergencies - a stupid idea which was now making sense.

The tube was stifling. A dog licked itself inside and out. A courting couple tongued each other's faces in an attempted fit of passion. It was hot. Bright stark lights illuminated the underground advert campaigns, which provided no relief from the claustrophobia. Some drunk leered over triumphantly catching everyone's attention as he nearly fell off the carpeted seat. I hugged my folder with the rules like a shield protecting me in battle. Then the inevitable happened, the train jolted to a bumpy stop and the lights flickered in film noir style. We were stuck. The drunk got up and ricocheted across the gangway before he took a piss in the crack partition between the two adjoining cars. I stared at the man opposite me hoping he might be able to save us all. He stared back blankly, and it all became rather uncomfortable, until he provided the diversion by pretending to wind up his bright submarine yellow digital watch. I chanted a mishmash of Madonna lyrics and religious sound bites: 'Thank You', 'Ray of Light', 'This Day', 'Loaves of Bread', 'Life is a Mystery', 'Amen'. Wondering how relaxed they would be on the rule of lateness. Slowly, very slowly, the train pulled out and shunted along. Another eight stops to salvation - Euston... Camden... Chalk Farm - tumbling from the underground... lift or stairs... lift or stairs... Come on, come on. The spiral walkway curled snail shaped to street level where I picked up speed on the ascent. Daylight blinded me as I leapt out of the proscenium arch building, and cut through the glass panelled bus shelter. Left was clear, right was clear. Turning the last corner, I ran to reach the central reservation that divided the large road. Without warning there was total silence and all I could see was black.

The sound of an ice cream van intensified, as a young man dressed in bulging orange cycling pants approached earnestly and repeatedly asked if I was alright. Something of consequence had happened and spectators were gathering. In no time at all an ambulance pulled up releasing two paramedics who without hesitation scooped me off the pavement and secured me into the back of the vehicle. The cyclist briefly climbed in behind us and although, exceptionally fit, he looked terrified. In a brief second, he told me very quietly that he was incredibly sorry, that he had no papers, and that he had to go, then like an apparition - he disappeared.

The corridors in the Royal Free Hospital, were crowded with beds parked up. For some folk this little piece of real estate was their home for the next few days. The estimated wait time in A&E was four hours. Lying unceremoniously in my swimsuit, that was now beginning to itch, on an NHS trolley, I could feel intense burning sensations running up and down my collarbone. The cone shaped translucent brace masking my face wasn't helping and I began to wonder if I would die like this, abandoned in Hampstead in a hospital with a bucket around my neck.

If I was going to die I would prefer it happened in Hong Kong so I had the chance of being exported out of the window where my spirit would be set free. From experience of working in old people's homes as a teenager, I knew those who died during the night were wrapped in tarpaulin and left in the porch for collection. I knew dying here would reek of the same lacklustre.   I started praying again - second time in one day, as you would in times of need - regretting that I hadn't bothered to do so more regularly as it might reduce the chances of now being heard.

Doctor Subramanian told me I was lucky to only have a broken nose and cracked ribs. The swelling on the eyes would reduce in time as would the bump to the head. The x-rays showed no damage to the spinal cord. He told me not to wear anything tight against my face, which meant no spectacles, no sunnies and no goggles. No goggles? Would that mean, no skiing? It's not like I went skiing but you know when something is taken away from you? The bruising would last for six weeks, and that I was lucky. Lucky? The charm bracelet I had been fondling as worry beads whilst the doctor talked now seemed part of a cosmic joke. The Miracle Buddha, the American Indian feather, the Phoenix. Was this karma biting me back for something? Why had I been chosen specifically to be ploughed down by an illegal speed freak?

An Amazonian looking nurse called Shonna with electric green eyes and curls of auburn hair came to assist with the last detail for the release form - handing me a nose bag to capture the last drops of blood as they dripped down my face.

Name: Zoe Sender.

Doctor's Surgery: Balham High Road, Balham

Age: 29

Date of birth: 8th August 1970.

Shonna suddenly stopped writing and smiled at me with an angelic sympathy as if she possessed a profound method of healing me on the spot.

'One hundred days until your thirtieth! My daughter's your age - it is a very difficult time. It's your Saturn Return.'

I stared long and hard at her. What now? What could I possibly be targeted with now? An imaginary ticker flashed all known medical conditions in front of me until I could only stop it by grappling with the words to ask what the hell was Saturn Return.

'Oh, in astronomy, every twenty-nine years the planet Saturn orbits the sun returning to the exact position it was at the time of your birth. It's a coming of age, re-birth if you like?'

Words were tumbling from Shonna's mouth. A mouth that had been savaged by years of smoking; tiny age scars ran riotously from the base of her nose to the top of her lip. I focused on the black frame of her comedy shaped glasses which moved in tandem with her ears as she spoke. A ladybird had settled on the left frame. There was nothing between us except for the damp stench of stale coffee and fag breath. She went on to explain that astrologically it is a time of confusion, challenges, doubt, fear, and hard lessons through which you learn to gain maturity, responsibility, significance and that the thirtieth birthday is a major rite of passage; deemed as the real start of adulthood.

'You're through the worst of it now though, once you hit thirty you should be fine.'

The impact of what she said hit me with more force than that of the cyclist whose crash helmet had beaten me black and blue and shocked me more than the damage his handle bars had inflicted onto my ribs. Standing alone in this hospital ward I understood what had just happened. Saturn, which was extensively a part of my DNA, without warning, without excuse, had vanished. I finally understood the power of goodbye. I was incomplete; an unfinished person. My life poured down on top of me. Saturn had gone, and I had to find a way to bring him back for my thirtieth birthday. I had one hundred days, and I had to be smart about it. I needed a life plan, with clear goals, and action focused strategies and a new way of thinking. Time was running out and there was a lot to achieve.

The first thing I did was get my hair cut.

A new look. It would serve me better than being late to the retreat, and I had far greater things to deal with now. I had to bring Saturn home.

Perhaps it was a small coincidence that a few days before this accident, Scarlett my ten-year-old god daughter, had plastered her ceiling in day-glow illuminous stars. She introduced me into a whole new way of thinking about my own interior design. I love the way people draw you into a new perspective. Painters bring you closer to colour and texture, doctors to bodies, packing designers to phallic shaped, everyday products. Scarlett took time with each pattern formation she was making as I heaved her closer to (her) sky each cluster represented something familiar to her. She painstakingly explained all there was to know about the constellations and planetary formation all of which she had picked up from her parents.

Adults never used to explain things as much, or as well, to children as they do today. Today is all about oversharing. It used to be little information with absolutely no negotiation. You either did as you were told, or you got a slap, unless you were fortunate enough to have been sent to a Steiner school, and then you could draw on the walls. After repeatedly pushing the clunky TV buttons from BBC1 to BBC2 to ITV over and over to find something of interest my dad would yell,

'Read the bloody paper!'

At six this was a huge ask. Staring hard at the print for too long, the words seemed to move like an army of insects across the page. By the age of eight I had lost all interest in what the papers said but had become a huge fan of Gerald Scarf. I understood later it was the TV listings my father was referring to and not the entire newspaper. Parents are like that, they give you bullet points then it's as if they expect you to run for Parliament with the help of a three-legged table and a box of chewed up pens.

Scarlett told me that Saturn is the second largest planet in the solar system, the sixth furthest from the sun. Its magnetic field is surrounded by a system of rings consisting mainly of ice particles. Saturn is named after Saturnus; Roman God of agriculture and harvest.

On further investigation I discovered the connection between agriculture and growth suggested that his lessons were manifested only over time. Hmmm, a patience game. I understood. Saturn represents our limitations whilst at the same time is our inner mentor and as we learn, we go through inner rebirth and enjoy spiritual growth. It was sobering to realise I had been so neglectful that I was stalling my own development. It was time to take responsibility for my actions.

I would need to woo him, seduce him and win him back.

So why did Saturn leave me? I couldn't help questioning this. We all know not to look back. No regrets... Live in the present... There are no mistakes.

So why?

Why?

Why?

Clearly it was a timing thing. Isn't it always? Want someone who doesn't want me? ... But without him I am incomplete... Darn it. Seems I was stuck in the hinterland of nowhere. It was time to visit someone who may have some clues.

****

Edie lived in hilly, leafy Highgate. Sitting opposite me like a picture of a traditional Welsh doll with her raven black hair and large, dark chocolate button shaped eyes, I watched as she peered down at my sweaty palms - scrutinising the lines that mapped out the details of my life. Cupping my hands in hers she gave them one almighty squeeze and then began to rub away at some of the marks already embedded like fossils deep into the skin.

'Ooowe your life ain' 'arve long, but there's a lot of 'assle going around ya. What's with the bruised eyes? You in pain?'

'Yes, my ribs are sore'

'No! You got an achin' 'art? Owwe! for goodness sake don't let it get t'ya, but are ya pregnant? You're not maternal though but children luv ya! Why don't ya think you can't 'ave none? Well, I know ya can and you've been worried about it, you 'ave bin thinkin' "God, if I leave it too late and don't get married quick, if I don't meet somebody, I ain't never gonna 'ave a family." Am I right? Well, that's you. Good innit? Now, I'm looking at your job 'ere and you seem fed up of it - cheesed off with it - it's a good job!'

'I am well, doing some consultancy work, freelance sort of…'

'But it's not you, are it? Where I'd like to see you is bein' a nurse. Honest to Gods you are so good with carin' for people, you got the bedside manner, ya so calm but ya always said, "I'll never get there".'

I stared blankly at her stunned into silence.

'But you're a lady who should be workin' for 'erself this is where I see ya! What is goin' on with you sweet'art because it's confusin' you somethin' terrible?'

'Hmmm' I mumbled.

'Ahy? You've been 'ere a little while y'know?'

'Hmmm…'

'What you are is in ya blood. It was in you the day you were born. But you've come this far. But what I'm gonna say to you is 'ave you bin offered somethin' right now?'

'Everything's up in the air basically' I confessed.

'Everything with you?' Edie fixed me with a beady look.

'Yeah, like everything is ouff…'

'Everything is gone?'

'Well…it's just…it's all…'

'Muddled!' She declared, triumphantly.

'Muddled, yes!' I conceded.

'Come on girl, 'ang on in there a bit longer. Go swimmin'. But I am goin' to tell ya something now. This year has bin a bloody awful year for you.'

I confirmed it had been rubbish.

'Rubbish! Not a penny, not a bloody sign of a bit of money comin' in - but '89 can you remember what you were doing? - You were working. You were here, there, everywhere and I know you feel "My God, time is passin' me by and I 'ave got t'be sortin' myself out soon."'

'I am actually looking for something' I explained.

'Yes! You 'ave got to start now before it's too late. If y'don't, you could be destroyin' things. Who's Snuggles?'

'Ugh. We had a rescue dog called Snuggles when we were growing up' I admitted.

'Jeez, why's 'e come into it? Why did 'e come into it now? It's as if 'e's been thinkin' of you.'

'He was a bitch, actually.'

'It's 'ard work' Edie continued. 'Don't be sayin' "I'm goin' on a diet!" Leave the tablets alone -you don't touch those pills. You got a strong body an' nice big arms an' legs. Strong. I mean that. I picked you up well darlin' nobody's told me about you. Your Grandmother's around you she says you remind 'er of 'erself - never listen - but she ain't 'arve proud of ya she knows you is fiery and you get emotional. Why is it you cry? An' I see your Grandad... How did your Mother feel - she thought she was 'avin' a boy?'

'Hmmm.'

'You're a tomboy aren't ya? You like to climb trees and play with the boys. You were the roller skate kid. Ten years ago, you could 'ave done it, you could 'ave found your way... Where were you then?'

'I was living in Hong Kong and travelling through South East Asia.'

'Now there's a man, he's not lookin' for a beautiful person an' you've got an honest face. He is lookin' for someone... he can't stand silly bitches... But he could be here sooner than you think. But I am goin' t'bless you and make your dreams come true. I can see Australia all around you but you've got an achin' 'art. You must take care of legs and feet - when you can put 'em up - I mean it. Look after those feet! Don't get bored, plod along. It ain't you - you deserve a bit of luck. What's his name?'

'Sorry?'

'Him. The one who's left.

What's his name?'

'Saturn?'

'Satan, he's got a bit of foreign in him I can feel it...' she puzzled. 'He'll be back. Good innit! Didn't expect that did ya?'

****

<u>1989</u>

Boracay a mango papaya island, in the Philippines; a paradise beach resort where the sand is as soft and smooth as baby powder, and the sea doubles as a looking glass. This was a time in the late eighties when there were no concrete duplex conferencing suites with air conditioning, and no sign of stressed out corporates drinking themselves into oblivion.

These were the undiscovered days when sheer happiness was staying in a dilapidated bamboo hut, with only sarongs as decoration, where travellers spent their days as if Robinson Crusoe himself.

Rita and I were both escapees from Britain when the economy slumped and there was a huge stench of hopelessness on every street corner. We both passionately wanted to be where the sun was shining, and where there was a sense of enthusiasm for the future.

Rita was a petite woman with an over flowing chest. Her dark hazelnut hair had a wiry energy to it that matched her sharp green eyes. She was a brilliant companion and, away from family, the roots of the friendship ran deeply between us. Rita was, however, very opinionated about politics and about conglomerates destroying the planet, media corruption, and the evil perils of globalisation.

A noble opinion diluted by double standards and a total lack of social responsibility when it came to conducting her own life. For this reason, it was always a relief to meet another kindred traveller when on long haul voyages to avert the conversation away from these contentious issues. Without diversions, I became Rita's sounding board. Muted and afraid to challenge her beliefs for fear of shattering her own self illusion, I took the wrap for all the wrong in the world. It was exhausting – the endless dialogue about the demise of Great Britain; flanked by the sound track of Morrissey, and Elvis Costello, yet at the same time it gave us a crusade and made us part of the cause.

An earthquake which hit Manila like a shaken snow globe had forced us to leave for the beach much earlier than intended and there was a great sense of foreboding as we drove out of the city paralysed by brown outs. We spent time applauding our decision to head towards the sea and we marvelled at how wise we were to do so. The journey was straightforward apart from an increased number of policemen; jumping jeepney to jeepney with the stealth of orangutans. We ate from roadside food vendors and took it in turns to sleep as the truck journeyed on. Arriving safely, we caught a catamaran to White Beach on the Western side of this dog-bone shaped island, which was surprisingly completely deserted and devoid of foreigners.

There, we learnt there had been much more than just an earthquake. It appeared we had just travelled through a coup plot against the Aquino government. The tourist resorts were deserted, it seemed the transport system had now been seized and the capital was at a standstill.

Boracay was deserted, however, it was not the military invasion alone that had caused the long stretches of white sand to remain empty. We had unwittingly managed to arrive on the same day television was tuned in to this remote beach resort.

Witnessing this event was both mesmerizing and alarming in equal measures as the screen flashed bloody news bulletins across the spectators faces. This tiny island was growing up fast and it gave Rita all the justification she needed to lament that TV was brainwashing innocent people. Villagers of all ages were transfixed by the twenty-four-inch screen - caught in a moment. Teenagers dressed in ripped Levi jeans, accessorised with red bandanas like pirates waiting to hear where the treasure could be found, watched in earnest as the pixels shaped into photographic moving images, the sound resonated through tall majestic palm trees that stood together like a herd of giraffes. The elders of the village stared in bewilderment as they watched the world they inhabit change, in front of their eyes. Children peered boldly at the screen as the images flashed silvery blue reflections into their eyes. Apart from the day Elvis died, I had not seen so much interest or emotion directed at a television.

That night on this isolated beach island we indulged in our nightly ritual of a cup of condensed milk tea and roll ups, inhaling the lingering fumes of mosquito repellent, laying like beached whales on our bamboo stilted beds. Our bodies were warm from the day's sun, it was the kind of evening heat that smothers you like a body stocking. All that could be heard was faint laughter in the distance, slightly muted by the sea, as it raised itself back and forth.

Clouds of smoke danced wildly towards the sky, beyond which the stars blinked like tiny crystals in the blanket of dark night. It was here in the privacy of these moments when the radiant sun had slipped past the rising moon as if kissing each other goodnight, that we started to reveal our own secrets, that by day we hung on to like hostages - fearing for their release.

'...Not happy... ...I left him... ...off work... ...sent home... ...chicken pox... ...bored... ...making jewellery box.... ...giant match box... ...sea shells... ...home early... ...didn't expect me there... ...he came in with him... ...spraying a fan shaped shell gold... ...new love... ...not so new... ...an affair... ...bisexual... ...I left him. Back to Jake... ...he left me... ...new girlfriend. Back to David... ...loved David... ...moving on... ...Japan or Ireland?... ...MA or MBA?... ...New Zealand...

...not the Philippines.... ...family... ...find my roots... England? ...Tea in the garden... ...summer time... ...didn't have a garden... summer love... ...England... ...freshly cut grass... ...missing England... ...I want to leave... Did I tell you I am taking up the guitar?'

I briefly reflected on Rita's confession... As kids we would screech with delight when diagnosed with 'catarrh' and would chase each other around the house practising air strumming on each other's chest in the knowledge we were about to embark on at least one week off school. Rita was always consumed with finding someplace other than wherever she was. I didn't understand her desire to escape. Was the burning insect repellent coil infusing toxic gases affecting her thinking?

We were in paradise away from the

earthquake, the coup, the recession, responsibilities. Even the television was now airing the soap opera Pangako Sa 'Yo (My Promise to You).

Why was Rita still on this continual search for a better place to be? Wanting a better life than the one she was currently living? What was it with people in their late twenties that made them so relentless, and unhappy?

It was clear that with age comes sadness and a deep rooted innate refusal to believe that what you have is good. Listening to her was like listening to a government radio station, where if you interrupt, the narrator cannot hear you and will continue to talk over you so that in the end you are forced to be quiet, as their voice will out speak you long before you could spurt any pearls of reason into the thread.

I admired Rita and her spirited nature but this incessant refusal of accepting her own happiness was not the best of her. I made a promise to myself there and then to be happy and that I would never be like this. With ten clean years ahead of me at the age of nineteen I knew it wouldn't even be part of my psyche. I had plenty of time to 'get things right' and my Nan always said, I had youth on my side.

Unknown to either of us, everything was about to change. Before our dreams had time to arrest us, Rita awoke wracked in pain; an abscess on her wisdom tooth growing to a mountainous size and her face transforming into pineapple proportions.

We left in darkness by catamaran to the main island that housed the nearest doctors surgery. The night sea was cold and threatening as we travelled with local fishermen returning from a night's work.

Clinging together we all held on to the spine of this scorpion like vessel. As if caught in a Pina Bausch dance, we endured the rocking motion of the tide as it beat the sides of the boat when the wind picked up speed.

It seemed like hours later when we arrived. In true middle of no-where style we were told the doctor was not at home and might return tomorrow… or the next day… or that week… or later that month…

We had no choice except to sit and wait.

The stark brightness of morning revealed there was only one roadside cafe. Decorated with dark, heavy, wooden colonial furniture the tables and chairs were spread out like a chessboard. A flea-bitten dog lay scared and maimed and panting in a collapsed state on the dirt track floor. A halo of flies furiously hovered overhead hoping to catch some vegetation from its open wounds.

As the heat increased, we became delirious and surrendered to its pressure by falling asleep; a sleep so deep it soothed like a lover's embrace. Hours passed like seconds, and the day came and went.

As we drifted in and out of delirium, it became apparent that we were now travelling along a make shift road in a truck. I had slept myself into unconsciousness as my stomach wrestled with itself, and during the day had developed a temperature in the heights of a raging fever.

Rita, in contrast, had experienced a small miracle. Having slept off the torture of her abscess, and armoured with the Valium she had scored on route, she was out of pain. We were taken to a church adapted into a medical centre of sorts. I was wheelchaired into a small white room - the vestry - which was empty apart from a large kidney shaped bowl that took prominence in the centre of the room. The medic pointed at the container and as she caught a flicker of resistance in my eyes she seized open my mouth and poured thick yellow liquid down my throat. Then as fast as she had done so, she left, leaving me alone with the shiny tin.

Singing echoed through the corridors I could hear Rita amidst the vocal ensemble. It was comforting at least as an underscore to my drama as they delivered the news that I had a rampant amoeba growing inside me like an alien. We were told we would need to get to the nearest city immediately, as this living organism needed to be expelled and the required treatment was so obviously unavailable in a church.

We made our way back to Manila,

returning through the chaos of natural disasters. An explosive cocktail of earthquake and typhoon that was heightened by political unrest in an attempted sabotage of the current government. As we entered Pasay City the split came. Rita decided to reduce her life to one deep purple back pack. Then dressed in her best outfit; a black cheese cloth shirt covering black shorts with her favourite dirty white plimsolls, she set off to find herself. The last memory I had of her was her hazelnut wiry hair cascading over her silhouetted, beetle like figure as she disappeared down the street.

Rock Water

Once a king,

always a King,

once a Knight,

is enough

(Dad, 1980)

On reflection, it seemed some things that Edie mentioned had resonated, and I knew to move forward I would need to enlist the help of some friends.

Kate and I had shared a wobbly wooden table at primary school. We had great seats at the back of the class where we could relax, and swap Love Is… stickers away from the glare of the teacher. Later, we briefly lived together in a flat share in Battersea with a fantastic view of the imposing and impressive power station. Kate moved to Brighton with her drummer partner Abel where she set up drumming circles for frustrated business executives trying to get in touch with their primal self. It would be lovely to spend time with her. The answer machine revealed Kate had left for Cambodia on a last-minute visit and wasn't expected back for another few months. Oh.

I tried Jade. Max picked up saying she had gone back to her family in St. Lucia, and that he didn't know what to do with himself. Anna was pregnant again, with only nine months between the last child, she said she was in the middle of a house move.

I spoke with Ben whose papers had arrived approving immigration to New Zealand and he was busy finalising his life in London. Rosa was setting up her own online spa business and was dealing with interfering investors. Fleur had landed a top job for a recruitment firm in the city and lamented that she had no 'life-work-balance.' Megan was recovering from a wake boarding accident and didn't want to leave the house nor accept visitors. Syd was moving to Spain with Julio and was in the midst of organising his life stuff, and Georgie had opened a small lounge bar in West Norwood, tipped as the new up and coming place to be. Hard to believe, I know. What was this trick of time where everything was changing, and people's journeys were fluid and evolving. People were moving on. Everyone, except me. I called Monique. She sounded sad and was available.

We met in the Tongue N Groove bar in the back streets of Brixton where they served expensive drinks. Monique was a friend from Hong Kong, who'd lived in the same apartment block in Causeway Bay before the landlord sold the flats to a property developer and everyone had to vacate. We shared memories of infamous joint raucous parties where people would rock up and stay until the music stopped, which meant we were always in a perpetual state of jet lag as a party could last up to a week at a time. The apartment became the hub for all wanderlust travellers who were not on expat packages and thought of the city as their home. Monique - an accessories designer - was doing incredibly well. One of her handbags had just picked up a gold at an Independent Handbag Awards in New York and had since featured in a popular US chick-com which was creating a whirlwind of success around her. Monique was the epitome of class and elegance, she had the gait of a rare and beautiful bird, and she always made you feel like life was full of joy. It was interesting to hear what she had been experiencing in the two years leading up to her thirtieth birthday. Two years my senior, she admitted everything had been plain sailing for her and that life in fact was proving to be easier and easier.

I wanted to explain to her my Saturn Epiphany, but the difference of experiences stopped me in my tracks. Comfortingly we did discuss the speed of life, that being in your thirties was merely the run up for forty - which is the wrong side of fifty and then the national retirement age kicks. If you encapsulated the time spent between now and birth you could equate it to several memorable birthdays when you got your first of everything; first tape recorder, first bike, first round of piercings, escapism from education, lots of kissing, drinking, and a few hilarious road trips with interesting people. If you did all that again for the next thirty years, taking you to the point of retirement, how far would you have really come? Knowing that those 'firsts' are replaced by advanced versions of things; gadgets, car, house, possessions.

It was here in this conversation between a coffee chilli martini and a vodka sky when nearly almost all the almond, cashew and hazelnut mix had been devoured, that Monique dropped the bombshell. Rafe, her brother, and a successful owner of an online games company had killed himself. He had taken the train to Eastbourne, then a bus from Duke's Drive to Belle Tout lighthouse, and at some point, along Beachy Head, had got up and walked out on his life. Rafe was at the peak of his success. Paradoxically it was disclosed in the aftermath of his death that he was crippled with debt and had been suffering chronic depression for some time. It was a complete and total shock. No one knew how much he had been suffering.

In tribute to his life, a small group of his close friends arranged a farewell gathering. He had always said he would like to be cremated and his ashes scattered into the sea. It seemed that this gathering should be in honour of his wishes.

In Hong Kong, Rafe was known as the DJ Junk, as he excelled at bringing everyone together for Junk Boat parties in the South China sea - never really satisfied until he had ensured all his friends had swam, barbecued, rested, laughed and listened to music at some hidden beach location, before slowly steering the boat back towards the neon city in time to catch the interchange between night and day.

A few days later, Monique and I agreed to meet inside a supermarket at Kings Cross train station to take the train out to the coast. The shop was bustling full of busy professionals, frantically rushing to get lunch meal deals ahead of the day, amongst tourists who were stocking up before they departed out of London. The deli stood out obtusely, dead meat, dead animals, arranged on an icy slab dressed decoratively with fresh garden herbs. An old man shouted as he waved two bottles of soda - his line of enquiry to see if there were any more on offer. I wanted to ask him if he had any idea what was happening today. Looking at his shrunken body with its tyres of skin hanging like an unwanted piece of jewellery around his neck, with stale alcohol exuding from his pores, it was clear that every day for him was a challenge.

We bought so much food that the rucksack pulled on Monique's shoulders - making her back contort under the heaviness. I shared the burden by wearing the rest in a bag around my waist, carried like a baby in a sling. A dilapidated train shunted us out of the hustling city. These tired trains were a rarity and somehow added to the gravity of the day. Litter carpeted the carriage floor. Remnants of other people's lives, scattered with tiny sparkling particles of glitter, like ashes now just dust on the ground, reflecting happier times.

A small group of us met at Digby's pub in

Broadstairs before moving down to the beach. The merriment of the pub eased us into the task ahead before we trekked down to the water's edge. The beach had clearly been used as an addict's dustbin - the meeting point where the last drops of sewage were injected into the vastness taking the syringes with it - clung to the sea bed like a deflated fishing net. An outbound tide secured us the freedom to climb into the sea caves away from the beach, where each of us dropped a single rose into the water as a personal farewell. One or two thorny stems fell into a rivulet that had begun to form between the rocks, whilst the rest glided out of the cave into the ocean. The openness of the isolated beach drew a serene tableau to the day.

Without explanation, Rafe had left us all, and here, now, was our chance to say goodbye.

When something bigger than you happens, it puts things into perspective, and surrounded by friends, I no longer wanted to share my news of waiting for Saturn to return.   Clearly the experience of death was a bigger reality than my own existence. In amongst my tears and the sadness, I experienced a slight twinge of happiness because death can make you appreciate the fact you are alive.

The trains were running a poor service that took double the journey time going back. Imagine being twenty-nine years old and so inept? Twenty-six pick-up sticks, twenty-nine hang your knickers on the line. Why couldn't I have driven Monique home in my open top Mercedes? Because I didn't have one. Why couldn't she come back and stay in my spare room (with its proper bed?) Because I rented a room with cheap carpet tiles and Lino and slept on a rickety futon, with a cat who had almost abandoned me.

****

Continuing with my research, the self-help manuals were a difficult read. Epic bible length narratives from *How to Heal Yourself, How to Heal Your Family, Do You Love Too Much?* and *Finding Love. The Man in Your Life is a Wolf, Your Mum Always Wanted You to be a Banker, The Feminine Psyche and How to Enjoy Sex at lunch time...* Each manual was very time consuming with no short cuts, that not even reading the back pages shed any light on being complete. The case studies appeared academic. I furiously searched for the *Dummies Guide to Getting Saturn Back,* it didn't exist. Yet. Where were the answers? Seriously, must one have to trawl through another person's misery only to discover they too are searching for the self-same thing?

I was in a relatively new relationship that was proving more challenging than it should be. Curiously, Asha showed enormous interest in the voluminous reading I was doing, so much so, I found myself cross referencing his name in various bibliographies just to make sure he hadn't penned any of this angst himself. We had both been invited to a mutual work colleague's wedding prior to becoming 'friends.' I had a growing instinct we wouldn't make it beyond a few weeks let alone to the ceremony.

'Angel I'm sorry, I will have to go and help her look for Milo' Asha announced on the phone one night.

'Milo, her cat?'

'She's upset' he explained.

'And you're upset?' I confirmed.

'I wish you wouldn't try to second guess

what I'm thinking…'

The phone beeps and I am on pause.

'Look, I'm not about to pretend I didn't have a past just because I am with you now. I am still very close to her' Asha sounded irritated.

I could begin to feel my teeth clench together as I responded with 'Right'.

'She's upset now. She's like you, and she is going through what you're going through…'

'I don't understand?'

'The whole soul-searching thing. She sat for two hours the other day outside my house crying' he revealed.

'Outside your house?' I exclaimed.

'I was out' he countered.

'Right.' I said again.

'Yeah, that's why I went over to her place later and put her to bed.'

'Put her to bed?' my eyes widened into the telephone receiver.

'Yeah, I made her a cuppa tea and put her to bed…'

'You slept with her?'

'I'm not sure I need this' Asha sighed.

'I agree - she sounds like hard work!'

'No. This… Us…' he floundered.

'What?' I asked.

'I don't know…'

'How long have you felt like this?'

'I don't know…'

'How long?'

'It just came to me then… I felt it then…

It's clearer when I speak to you - this is too complicated!'

'I'm complicated?'

'No,' he confirmed. 'I am saying WE are complicated – together.'

Silver lining: In that moment I realised I needed to make this journey alone. No more diversions. I knew it was time to make 'the list'. The list is something we are often told to do, but never bother doing. 'They' say it really, really helps to put pen to paper.

Number One: Stop dating men who were still in love with someone else; whether it be a girl they saw in the playground when they were five and rejected them, a girl they once saw in the street and fell in love with immediately but have never seen again (yawn,) or a real life proper ex-girlfriend.

Number Two: Avoid the Serial Leaver who is still avenging his first love walking out on him. Here you really are just a casualty in someone else's war.

Number Three: Avoid the Philosopher with wonderful theories on how to live life (often not equipped with right tools to do anything about them.)

Number Four: Avoid the Manic in Remission. He will love his own sense of morality and will always adore alcohol more than he will ever love you.

Number Five: Avoid the Workaholic who is fun for the first flush of meals and holidays, but you will never be a priority over his gadgets as he is permanently plugged in elsewhere.

Underneath 'the list' I drew a line and created my own affirmations:

'I am a happy single woman.'

'I am a happy single woman
enjoying life.'

'I am a happy single woman who's
enjoying life and staying single
until her Saturn Returns.'

****

Missing the train from Euston limited the chance of getting to Scotland in time for the wedding and the only viable route was to take the very last National Express from Victoria. Hanging out with the late-night winos at the bus station, I devoured several cans of lager before alighting the coach, in the hope that it would help me sleep through the overnight ride up North. An ill-advised plan as I spent most of the journey in the toilet trying to defy gravity as the bus heaved its way through the

heavy traffic out of London and on to the M11.
The only saving grace was that the darkness of
the night ride created an incubator for the
weary travellers and time passed without all
the bright bulbs and frequent stops of a train
journey. We arrived on time with the sun
rising across the city. It brought with it the
perfect conditions for a day of celebration and
tribute to love.

Waiting for me at the other end was Kylie -
red faced and seething with rage. Tom, her
long-term boyfriend had left her and would
not be attending the wedding either. I was so
happy that we had a shared experience but
knew she wouldn't see it that way. We agreed
that she should stay off the booze to avoid any
attempts to 'share' her situation with the other
guests. This day was all about hope and
new beginnings and we both knew it would be
inappropriate to divulge thoughts and feelings
on anything to do with failed or doomed

relationships. I affected an enthusiastic tone suggesting that we should look forward to the day's celebrations marvelling at how this could be the perfect tonic for both of us.

Despite our best intentions to be jubilant and supporters of love, if there is one event to make you feel to the core that you have a dysfunctional relationship streak in your genes, it's someone else's wedding. If you're not immediate family and within the inner circle of activity you can feel isolated. If you are in the inner circle you feel dislocated by the mass of strangers attending what you deem as a private event. Either way you are lost. The pressure for everyone to enjoy themselves and for all feuds to be set aside for a day creates an intensity and expectation, that can only really disappoint, in the end.

Weddings are like a piece of theatre, everyone wants to go and see a well devised play, with a good cast, great writing, brilliant set design, evocative music, a crowd pleaser, an award-winning performance. Kylie and I knew this wedding would be exceptional; the bride and groom were both from a long line of traditionalists who would not falter on any of the details, especially since these childhood sweet hearts had survived a long-term relationship with all its ups and downs into their late twenties and still loved each other. Truly.

The actual ceremony was held in a beautiful old church and was idyllic in setting, as it was in atmosphere. We chose to stay close to the back - safe enough for a quick exit if needed. Hymns, poems and a harpist lured us into the beauty of the event with a colourful fashion feast of rich and traditional fabrics, with feathers and flowers donned by the rest of the congregation. Next door to the church was the mansion house serving a lavish sit-down lunch with champagne on tap.

Everything seemed on track, right up until the best man's speech. Well, let's face it, it was always going to be the wild card of the day:

'I am very proud to be marrying off my best wee pal, Daniel. Never thought I'd see the day...' The room swelled with laughter. 'Before I start, I want to say we wouldn't be standing here today if it wasn't for a certain someone in the room today, and I want to thank you from the bottom of my heart for bringing these two together...' More murmurs and faint laughs started echoing around the great dining hall. 'This person will always be remembered as giving love a chance.'

'Awww' could be heard circling around the room, mixed with 'so, so, sweet'.

'I want you all to put your hands together in appreciation for our cupid, Kylie Delaware!'

Signalling to our table, the groom diverted everyone's attention. Most of whom started applauding with a few standing up whistling in delight. I was hot; burning with the embarrassment and trying to avoid this huge intrusion of privacy so frantically clapped back at the crowd. Kylie leapt with such urgency the wedding favours fell from the table, and without saying a word, she broke into a run.

Unfortunately, as with some cinemas, there was only one door at the bottom left of the room. Given that we were on a round table mid centre right she had to run a full circuit before she reached the top table and could exit out; leaving a bewildered best man holding court.

Kylie's outburst was met by icy silence as the tartan clad audience stared on in surprise. I rose apologetically and thankfully noticed a shut French window. Moving towards the window frame, the curtained upholstery fell like a wrap around my body in what looked like a tailored sari as I struggled to get out.

It must be said that there is something safe about French windows. A clear-cut route. A window with a door in it - how reassuring. Providing a broad view on the world so everything can be seen outside - with a smoke screen as to what is going on inside. As pre-teens, we would watch horror videos certificated eighteen, hosting regular video parties so our friends could watch films not sanctioned by their own parents. On one occasion, half way through a budgie having his head bitten off in *The Hills Have Eyes*, a dead mouse attached to a mousetrap in a tandem jump came hurtling down from an upstairs window. Dad, in his wisdom had decided whilst we were pre-occupied watching movies, he would deal with a field mouse that had come inside to live in the skirting boards between the bedrooms. At the time, all of us in this secret video club just sat there bewildered not knowing which was more alarming, the reality on the TV or what we had just witnessed through the panes of glass.

Outside, I was alone in the vastness of the hotel grounds. Surrounding every corner were amazing, panoramic views of the Scottish Highlands. Turning back, I could vaguely see what looked like the guests laughing in unison as the speeches continued. In the distance I caught a glimpse of Kylie running towards the edge of a mound leading towards the cliff top, where she appeared to be doing some form of shadow boxing.

Clambering after her, I regretted both coming to this wedding and for wearing a tight vintage dress, as it made for a difficult climb towards my friend. I put on my best 'give the gun to me' tone of voice and tried to coax her away from the cliff. At the same time, inching close enough to grab her waist, where I pulled her in so that she could collapse onto my chest, then as if in a rock 'n' roll dance, I spun her around and like a life guard at the deep end of a pool, I dragged her body weight to the surface of the small hill as she repeatedly giggled and hiccupped into my ear,

'Haven't bin drinkie.'

A path in front of us forked with two identical tracks. Like having an atlas with the locations missing, I would have to decipher which would be the best route to take. Kylie was clearly in no state to walk alone and was too heavy to carry. There was only one way around this. I tied her faux pashmina scarf around one of her ankles joining it to one of mine and in what was close to a two-legged race I pulled her in a zigzag fashion across the lawn towards the church car park.

Dusk was closing in and the light shifted, accentuating the beautiful golden and purple hues of a magnificent sunset. The Highland air had a damp freshness, which was a relief from the antics of the day. I had managed to find our way back through the main entrance of the hotel where I pushed the drunken mess into a small old-fashioned, wrought iron crated lift and up to the tiny bedroom away from the other guests, whilst giving myself time to change and freshen up for the evening's party.

A Motown tribute band had been booked and the second tier of party revellers were now arriving in their droves. A festive atmosphere was whipping up in and outside the building. Like a crafty parent escaping from a child with problems sleeping, I crept out of the darkened bedroom, safely making it to the door. As if on cue, Kylie rose from the bed staring at me with wide Bambi eyes and whimpered,

'You not going to leave me, are you?' and promptly burst into tears.

****

Dexter, had become my only confidant, and he didn't hide his scepticism. He said my theory about Saturn was not rational, but then he was a very rational person, so he would say that.

He was, however, an extremely talented musician who spent his days composing scores for television and film companies. We shared a large Victorian house in one of the wide streets that formed part of the Tooting Triangle. The house was divided into eight bedsits varying in size and shape. Each room broken down to a Lino, and a carpeted, surface area. The carpet denoted your living space, and the Lino the kitchenette. It was cheap chic caravan living. The house spanned three floors and each resident had to endure their neighbours to the right, and above as paper thin walls made for the sound effects of wounded rhinos walking about. Like any Victorian conversion, these houses were not intended for cosmetic reconstruction.

The only communal areas; the bathroom and toilet, provided little neutral space and although we solely inhabited these studio flats, the house felt every bit a home as it gradually filled itself up with friends of friends.

Since we two were the only freelancers, we spent most of our days together listening to and critiquing Dexter's music over a variety of toasted cheese sandwiches or Ryvita with marmite, and roll ups. His bedroom-come-studio doubled up as bachelor love shack with eclectic furnishings; an ensemble of presents acquired from lovers along the way. A midnight blue and purple long-haired rug formed a bedspread covering his mattress by day and transformed the floor by night. The rainbow coloured beaded curtains, the rubber plant, and the Moroccan style lamp shade in coloured glass with decorative metal, gave the room an exotic Middle Eastern feel.

It was during one of many of these toastie

sessions that Dexter suggested I should find a way of exorcising this madness out of me and speak to someone trained. He was giving me the push as he had a lot of work to finish with imminent deadlines he knew he couldn't continue as the sole bearer to what was now becoming my obsession. I knew that having a therapist was very much part of an emerging sub culture and that for some their relationship with their analyst was the longest relationship of all, but I had never attempted nor needed to go down this route, so felt perhaps now would be a good time to do so.

****

Megan greeted me at the door of the Stoke Newington clinic, dressed head to toe in white tunic and slacks, she beckoned me in to a room full of shoes. A signal then to go barefoot. We continued through an elongated kitchenette area to a small box room, a stark white heavenly set with moth coloured drapes covering a large back facing window. It smelt of burning wood and rosemary, perhaps to mask the smell of people's feet. A portable massage table irreverently stood in the centre covered in an unappealing grubby white towel. In the far corner were a set of wicker chairs facing each other, to the side a low table with a bowl of fresh fruit, a jug of water, a pair of cymbals, and an incense stick burning. Entering further into the room - with the enthusiasm of having a smear test - I began to have doubts about the situation. Megan headed towards one of the chairs and promptly sat crossed legged staring at me. I followed suit and attempted to squash into the remaining empty seat - taking time to lodge my body safely inside its wicker frame. The urge to giggle was exhausting. Minutes turned into what seemed like hours as we stayed like this - the silence only broken by the creaking noises as we moved our positions. My stomach began to ache from the tension, which caused a burning sensation as trapped air began to try to fight its way out.

Megan slowly started the rhythmic nod of a toy dog in the back of a car. Her neck seemed slightly elongated as it tilted forwards almost bowing towards me. This was expensive silence. It reminded me of being in confession in those primary years. That wretched silence. For those who haven't ever been to confession, the aim is to get you to tell the priest all your sins, so that you can repent and He (God) can forgive you. Usually with a few Hail Marys. The problem, as a child, was that you had to create something bad you had done to validate being in confession in the first place, knowing that if you confessed to anything too extreme - like you had murdered your family - you would be carted off by social services.

The only way to give your tale authenticity was to lie and say you hadn't done the washing up, your homework, or been nice to old people.

'What brings you here today, Zoe?'

Whether it was the pressure of the silence I don't know, but words came spewing out of my mouth. The prospect she might be able help find a solution to winning Saturn Return spurred me on to throw up everything that came to mind. After what seemed like a very short time she picked up the cymbals and clashed them together forcing the sound to echo around the room. She told me the session was over, that I should only do things that made me *feel* 'ok', that we had a lot of work to do, and that she recommended meeting once a week until further notice. She also said that things would get tough, and that I may not like what she had to say, that she would challenge me and we may fight.

I reflected on what she said. Not going back (ever again) felt 'OK.'

Island Wall

11 was a racehorse,

22 was 1 2,

1111 race and 22112

(Dad 1979)

'Meditation is good for spiritual awareness and heightened consciousness, and it only requires a quiet room.' On reading further, I understood meditating on an object like a burning candle, can help to concentrate as the flame attracts the eyes to increase your chances of focusing on a single object, and the light creates an impression on the retina that is stored in our memory when the eyes are closed, that illuminate consciousness. A quiet room, and a candle. Clearly it was time to meditate on Saturn Return. There had been no reward for my recent efforts of spending money on every single charity direct marketing envelope that came to the house and returning with donations; nor from the direct debit I had set up for both Comic Relief and Peace One Day; not even from all the clothes and books I had given away to the various charity shops that lined Clapham Common down to Balham High Road. It seemed as if no one could see just how hard I was trying to do things better and I needed some serious help on how to take this to the next level. Pulling my spine taut, pushing my shoulders down and back, I tried to relax. Relax and breathe. I tried to concentrate and let my thoughts disappear.

Doesn't silence amplify the slightest thing? The noises coming from the other bedsits formed a melody all their own. It was proving hard to push out this eclectic sound track.

Concentrate...

Con...

Cen...

Constantinople, Istanbul...

Opening the fridge door, the blue light illuminated my profile with sinister shadowing in the same way a lighted torch under the chin in the darkness can morph your face to appear eerie. It was empty apart from a tub of margarine, and a half empty bottle of vodka. Closing the fridge door only exaggerated the darkness as the flame barely gave off enough light. Taxi clumsily squashed her body through the door, stopping in her tracks and looking at me with an intense squint as she saw me sitting crossed legged on the floor, next to a fading light.

I fixed my glaze on the flame of the candle and placed my palms over my eyelids to block the light coming from under the door, noticing that the aqua marine coloured nail varnish did look better than the black lacquer the sales assistant had tried to make me buy. At least the varnish covered up the half-moon embossed on each finger as a direct result of lack of milk. Thank goodness for lactose free alternatives.

Relax and breathe. Try to focus on breathing and letting all other thoughts go. The smell of fig engulfed the room and tightened like a silk scarf around the neck. The smell did everything it could to intensify the hunger and make me tired. I tried to bring the image of the flame to my mind. Taxi walked across the carpet with the self-assurance of a super model and knocked the candle. Flames leapt up and caught a hand tied bouquet of dried roses hanging like a picture on the wall. The flames spread out like a fan and after throwing a wet tea towel at it there was nothing left but charcoaled petals and the stench of smoke.

As I opened the door to let the fumes out,

Taxi darted up the stairs to the safety of

someone else's room and I was greeted by Dexter in the hallway in his Japanese kimono dressing gown shifting uncomfortably from one foot to another: -

'Someone's been sick in the bath!'

Following him into the first-floor Romanesque bathroom I noticed how stark the light was compared to that in my own room. We both peered into the old-fashioned deep iron tub –

'That's not sick, that is the remnants of a fizz bomb.'

We got into a heated debate as Dexter noticed a wet towel hanging limply from the clothes horse and believed me to be the culprit of this mess. I told him I was trying to meditate and that he should have better things to do with his time. He went on to berate me saying the whole candle searching process was because I was uptight, that I should forget the vow of singledom, and that he liked me better when I was dating.

Inside my room, I returned to my books. I looked up 'fire' and it referred to passion and emotions, then turning to the back page of *How to Meditate* I read *Enjoy the Journey - It is More Important than the Destination.* Slamming the book shut, I decided to go out.

As Raul and I left the bar together, I realised that all these thoughts about turning thirty, had made me introspective and I had the overwhelming desire to be alone. We walked in uncomfortable silence both facing ahead as if acutely intrigued by something in the distance. To break the silence, he started to literally steer me across a main road pretending to drive me along as if I were a car. I looked at him in this moment of child's play and it dawned on me just how male Raul was. Here was a hot-blooded, attractive man walking me home, and I was, unprepared.

I realised that whilst I had been busy obsessing over Saturn Return, I had lost the ability to connect with the opposite sex. I knew I had to fill in the silence to avoid any more of this strained atmosphere, so I attempted bringing Raul into my thought process.

'You see, mermaids and fairies, are like your angels. Your "self." It's all about change and time. It's about the masculinity aligning with her feminine self. You see the ebb and flow. You will be confused and there are hard lessons. What I am trying to say is that, it is like the butterfly effect and one action shifts another in motion. Best not to fight it. It's your choice if you follow the path or the river.

It comes with maturity and responsibility.

If your moon is very strong in Neptune things will be very illusionary - could be addictive.

I'm not saying I am addicted. Need to be in tune with nature, well what's the point of being frozen, I mean it's cold and you must chill out at some point? It's the difference between having your feet bound like a concubine and wearing flip-flops. So, in the end it's mental slavery that wraps you in chains, but where's the key? The key is to your heart - if you believe it you will find yourself full of ambition and maturity - but you have to be patient and wait...'

All the time I was talking I remembered what Dad had taught us about being in uncomfortable situations, and that was to have a secondary back up plan to every situation. I knew by the time I had stopped talking that if Raul had a change of heart and tried to kiss me or invite himself in, I would slap him and let him know this was inappropriate. This would be my back up. Instead, he looked at me quizzically and then swiftly planted a kiss on the top of my head, did a three-point turn, and left.

I am not saying he was running – more speed walking. I couldn't believe it, like, what was his problem? Was I becoming untouchable? I marched home to let Dexter know his advice had been useless and that I should never have been forced back out into the dating scene but when I got inside he was busy entertaining a dancer, or he was dancing, and she was entertaining, I can't really remember. I just knew that on top of everything else I had now become socially inept and totally incapable of having a normal conversation.

****

There was something foreboding about the overcast sky as I trudged up the hill to Marilyn's flat in Wimbledon Heights. So, I began to focus on making a mental list of the things I could ask to be hypnotised for. I had read that sometimes in life an event happens to us where one of our personalities gets stuck or left behind. Rather like horses going around a horse track, as they go forwards one or other will fall behind or get rooted to the spot. Hypnotherapy is then a natural way for us to catch up to speed with ourselves, a chance for all the horses to meet and run along at the same pace. It can be used to change a person's behaviour, emotional content, and attitude, as well as a wide range of conditions including dysfunctional habits, anxiety, stress-related illness, pain management, and personal development.

Marilyn saw patients in her roof top flat that opened out with skylights projecting into the treetops below. Her home was designed modestly and given it was where she worked and lived, it was neither too homely, or too formal. There was a welcoming feeling as you entered. She ushered me to the living room and ask me to sit into position centre of the sofa where she gently forced me into the swell of the velvet cushioned upholstery whilst I tried my hardest to be as relaxed as I could.

'Simply follow my finger…'

What? Like, no pendulum?

'Keep following my finger.'

It didn't work.   I felt sorry for her and tried to think of distracting sobering thoughts to stop the urge to get lost in hysterical laughter Marylin's earnestness made me want to at least, try this.

'Think about why you have come here, and what you would like to change Zoe.'

I started to think about Saturn Return and the panic I had about running out of time, only two months until my thirtieth birthday, whilst watching her finger swinging from side to side.

'Down the stairs to a beautifullll - gardennnn... What do you see in front of youuuu?... After walking through the garden, you reach a - mirrorrrr... Oneeee... Twoooo... SMASH!'

I suddenly became aware that I was dribbling, and Marilyn was staring at me. She said we had finished, that forty minutes had passed, that I had had a terrible shock and that I needed something sweet to eat and most importantly I was not to talk about what had just happened for twenty-four hours and I must go home to rest. I felt exhausted, as if I had just run a marathon (not that I had ever run one before.) I was drained, and, unbelievably whacked out. Strangely enough I felt relaxed despite the fatigue. Getting off the sofa I found myself stretching in some absurd yoga poise I had once seen in a healthy lifestyle magazine.

I called Dexter on the way back down the hill to tell him I couldn't tell him anything for twenty-four hours. He didn't pick up, so I just blew a raspberry noise on his answer phone instead. The moody skies had cleared, and the sun was blazing through the huge white clouds. It seemed as if everyone was looking at me, whether it be the glow from my newly hennaed hair or if something magical had just occurred I wasn't sure, but either way I now knew my thoroughbreds were in the right place.

****

'I like your hair dear. Your brother had purple hair once when he was hanging around with that girl from Turkey. He was upstairs with a group of friends and she did it. Then he came down to show me. I said "Oh, that looks very professional!" But I thought "Oh dear!" Yes, they were sitting up there smoking that brown stuff... I called up "Sheldon, what are you doing?" And they came down in the end.'

I had so much in common with Nan. We were both single, lived alone, ate meals for one, and had a quest for adventure. You could tell Nan anything - she was a hoarder of family secrets. I confided in her about what Shonna the nurse had said and asked whether there was anything she could tell me about Saturn Return.

'Well yes dear, you should have come to me earlier. They said in the local... I've given it to your mother... They said several people who lived in different places saw two, not one, two over Whitstable. Well, I saw red in the sky. Because it was night-time I didn't take any notice but thinking now, it *might* have been the glow from the space ship. It's not far from here, Whitstable beach. I saw a red glow. They say they saw UFOs - you know - round like a saucer? Two of them. It was in the local paper... Your mother will show you.'

She continued, 'You haven't got the fire on have you dear? You must keep the door open or else it gets too oppressive in here. There, that could be something to do with your Saturn Return.'

I wasn't convinced that Nan's sightings of space ships really had anything to do with my search but told her that maybe it could be a sign.

'Everything is a sign dear. Look at that time I was on the street and everyone gathered on the beach... I dreaded being watched more than being frightened. We were so wet, and that dog nearly drowned because it was so small. I never went on that street again. Never... Would you like to sit here dear, you look very hot?... We were marooned - Beryl and I - we had her little corgi dog with us - he had little tiny legs. Beryl was always finding shells and stones and making things, so we were right at the end of the street and didn't notice the water had come in around us. Trust Beryl, she was one of these clever people too interested in what she was doing to be bothered with what was around her. I didn't know and when we looked up we were surrounded by water and everyone was looking at us from the beach. It was a fisherman's boat that rescued us in the end. They do a lot of rescues from the street especially in bad weather. In the war they used to say, "the weather was bad" - that meant they had no bread. She never fed that dog. I told you she was a boffin. She had two of them and she used to forget to feed them. One of them had to have an operation and when they opened him up they found all this material in his stomach. She used to do needlework and leave her things hanging about. Poor dogs! One of them ate a wasp once when I was there...' She carried on.

'Did somebody just come to the door? It might be Doctor Turner, when he last came around, he crouched down to talk to me and I forgot I was deaf, so I kissed him...'

Nan bit her bottom lip, and pulled a 'well, I never' grimace.

'That Cindy will be here any minute. They can't keep the help you know. They don't get paid enough - I'm sure they don't even make their fare to work. That Cindy she is an artful thing, she had the cheek to say to me,

"Have you got anything to tell your family?" I said "Yes, I slept with a mouse" and she said, "did you see the end of it?" I made light of it you know? I said, "I could never kill a mouse."

Only she keeps mice, you see? She said it was her lifetime ambition to look after animals and I know she brought one here one day, in a Tupperware bucket, a mouse! She has got three dogs, two cats, mice and what are these things that look like rabbits? These animals with hair… guinea pigs. I was sitting there waiting for her to finish and I saw something run past the television and I thought "Argggh that's a crab" but it was this mouse. You could tell it was well looked after. I was petrified and was ever so glad when she came in, but the cute thing, it saw the Tupperware bucket and it jumped in. "There!" I thought. "It must have come in that and knew where to go!" I mean, I could have been one of these who'd have a seizure.'

'Nan, are you sure...?'

'I said to her, "What colour are your mice?" and she said "Brown," and this was a brown one! I was furious at the time but now I see the funny side of it... But she must feel guilty as she said to me, "Have you got anything to tell your family?" That gave it away. Well, you asked me dear and I'm telling you.'

Maybe Cindy was onto something. If Saturn was to come back me, perhaps it was time to figure out my lifetime ambition.

****

Thud. The front door banged persistently. The intercom didn't work so if you strained your ear hard enough you could vaguely hear voices in the same way a caller in a poor signal area is heard on a mobile. Both were inaudible and disappointing if you expected full sentences. No one was due at the house and it could only be a nuisance caller, advocating politics or religion, or worse, the TV Licence inspector. The voices drew louder and peering at the glass door I could see the shadowed outline of two bodies. Proceeding with caution I prized open the front door. A burly woman in combat gear pushed past me, past all the recycled coloured sacks of rubbish, the stack of bicycles fixed to the walls like collectors' items in a modern art show, and sped up the stairs, followed by an insipid man in a suit. Then they both stared down at me from the banisters.

I had made it a ritual as a child that anything unwanted from my life would be left on the landing in my parents' house. It was an unspoken ritual between myself and my mother that any discarded, displaced object would be left out for her to dispose of. It was a way of getting rid of all my baggage. Craning my neck to stare back at those two I wished that they could somehow be collected and taken away. Averting attention, Dexter appeared in his running kit causing them to scuttle back down the stairs again in my direction.

'Zoe Sender, Flat 8?'

Staring hard at Dexter for some sort of support I hoped he would help entertain our new guests but instead exited out of the house.

'Housing Fraud department - we need to see your passport and bank statements…'

In a synchronised gesture they held up what appeared to be identity cards and they told me they were from Wandsworth Council, investigating housing fraud. I tried leaving them in the hallway whilst I crawled my way back up to my room; instead they followed, arriving before me.

The paperwork took time to find; hidden amongst old birthday cards tucked away between postcards and unpaid bills, name cards, travel articles I had never read - least of all bothered to travel to - and scraps of phone numbers on napkin and beer mats. It didn't seem to be enough to settle the situation and I found myself having to prove that the small space we were all now huddled in was, in fact, my bedsit, privately rented. I was close to asking them if they needed a urine sample, or perhaps they would like to sniff the sheets? Fortunately, photos hung around the walls like a gallery framing different moments of my existence and this seemed to settle them, whilst I continued to look for a tenancy agreement.

There had been a spate of housing benefit

frauds and random checks were being made in the local area. Whilst I hadn't been in receipt of benefit, I had been singled out from an old database, which was showing my name on their systems. Once the final checks were complete, the two withdrew from the room. Noticing the main front door was ajar when they left, after watching them shrink down the street I pulled it tight behind me.

Musing at the mound of paperwork, personal admin and letters that were now scattered across the bed, I decided to write to Saturn. The book said letter writing was one of the best ways to release negativity and to communicate in a more loving way. The first step was to download what was annoying you; to tell the person what they've got to say to you to make you feel better. I liked that part. Then you had to make sure you showed the person your letter and their response. Then your response to what they said, and their response to that... Or perhaps you stopped at their response? Basically, one of you should stop, or it becomes a chain letter.

The book guided through the process of constructing letters and provided key points along the way of things not to forget. Like, to remember the address of the person you were sending it to, to sign the letter so the receiver knew who it was from, and that in some situations a P.S. help - P.S. please reply!

Part of the process was to write down all the things you felt before you put pen to paper...

Anger: I am angry you left.

Sadness: I am sad that you don't want to be with me.

Fear: I am afraid. I don't know why you left.

Regret: I am sorry that you left.

Love: Let's be together; I love you.

Dear Saturn,

I've been waiting a long time for someone like you.

I will keep searching, as I believe that someday soon we can be together as one.

Cheers,

Zoe x

This exercise was interrupted by a high pitched shrill from the bowels of the house. A purple faced bedsit neighbour named Kimberly was running in and out of the rooms in what appeared to be a bedroom farce. Apparently, we had been burgled. All the TVs, DVD players, most of Dexter's studio recording equipment and anything remotely electronic had gone. There was chaos - the sort of chaos that went on into the night – repeated as each member of the house returned home. The only things left untouched was the attic storage room which was mainly full of empty suitcases, and my room. Although she never said anything directly to me, Kimberly was divisive, going between each housemate and trying to convince them that the only person at home whilst this crime was committed was potentially the number one suspect.

I wouldn't have minded so much if I hadn't seen them. The bitter chill from outside had caused the condensation to create a mist on the windows of the eateries and shops that sloped up the street to the house. All the housemates, as if in a picture postcard inside the warmth of our local lounge bar Gobblins, were surrounded by bottles of wine. Since the burglary they had taken to going out by invitation only, forming a bizarre exclusive member's only club, headed up by Kimberly. It wasn't ever mentioned but the silence when they were all out was enough to remind me I had been excluded.

The burglary had breathed an uncomfortable atmosphere into the fabric of the house and it no longer felt like the home it had once been. The fact we left the doors unlocked for Taxi to be free to roam became a topic of contention causing paranoia, so it was decided it was time to give Taxi the black and white cat, a more stable environment.

Preparing her for her change of living conditions, I cut up photos of my parent's garden and stuck them along the skirting boards to act as visual stimuli, hoping to lull her into her new world with ease.

With the housemates out, being alone with the phone was becoming dangerous – there are always friends offering services to one another in an opportunity to talk about life dramas. I tried not to get trapped in this habit, and, remembering Marilyn's bid to remain silent after the hypnotherapy session I tried to distract myself from going on a phone-athon.

The house needed a facelift. Age old ripped posters of rock stars hung lifelessly in the corridors, precariously dangling by pieces of glueless cellotape; the membrane of yesterday, and dust particles like bird droppings collected in the corners between each room. Who could forget their teenage first fixation with a pop star whose portrait would be honoured daily? The intensity of passion for someone you have never met, let alone had a conversation with, was incredible. The desire to go where they were, being prepared to travel nationwide or worldwide to see them. You idolised them for having the ability to make you feel you were the only one in a crowded venue, leaving you to float home love induced, where in the stillness of your bedroom you could lie on your bed with excitement in your stomach still hearing their music ringing in your head - providing the backing track to the next few teen years. I was convinced, utterly convinced, that I would elope at some point in my life with a music god.

Life for most in their twenties meant being on the move. Changing beds, trains and planes so frequently was exciting. Moving between hotel, to bamboo hut, to tent became the norm, whilst all the time secretly longing for a place to feel settled. This secret longing was devoid of the realities that searching for accommodation in the Big Smoke brought. It was complicated and expensively laden with landlords, tenancy agreements, rents in advance, deposits, the compiling of references, and trips to IKEA and hyped-up second-hand toot from vintage furniture shops.

To the right of our semi-detached we had noisy young children who screeched and cried early morning until late in the day. The house to the left sounded like they had sex on loop as the noises permeated through the walls. Gross. We were caught in the middle where drum and bass met Peruvian chant - and kid's nursery songs overrode Eddi Reader. The immersion heater sounded like an aircraft taking off, and the toilet cistern made a painful gurgling noise.

Living on top of each other meant there was never any real privacy. If someone was depressed, you all knew about it. If someone brought home a new squeeze, you all knew about it. If someone met you in the corridor with that furrowed brow 'we need to talk' expression, you knew you needed to grab your keys and be off. There were too few opportunities to avoid the wrath of your neighbours' idiosyncrasies. Isn't it fun to be financially and responsibility free? No, it's chaotic and exhausting - each person soaking up each other's lives with all their complications confusing your own personality with theirs. So, who is happy? People who live alone, support themselves, and pursue their dreams?

If there was one single benefit of living in a bedsit – it was you were self-contained. You didn't have the bother of going upstairs and downstairs to cook. With your built-in kitchen, you learnt there was a lot you could accomplish on a Baby Belington. It was not long before you forgot you were living in unnaturally cramped conditions and everyone settled into their new existence somehow learning to minimalise movements and reduce everything to dolls house size proportions. Falling down the lifestyle ladder you knew everything came at a price but at least this way you were free from responsibility. Yay.

The urge to escape was beginning to burn deep inside me and whilst all the time I had been in this fun co-operative style of living, I had enjoyed it, I knew a time would come to move on and find a place alone. Responsibility did seem to be creeping up on me quicker than I had envisaged and the happiness I felt previously, was now a burden.

I did what I always did when these feelings of change became like loud cymbals crashing in my ear - I went to bed. A cushioned retreat, a place where you could ponder uninterrupted on life. Before sandwiching my head between the pillows, I made a call:

'Welcome to the Leo Hotline. Here is your forecast for the week ahead… No matter how hard you try to solve a partnership issue it eludes you. Even if you think you're bashing your head against a brick wall, you must keep believing that the answer is out there somewhere, waiting to be discovered, because it is. Whilst it's not far away, it may be that you find the answer somewhere unexpected.'

That night, I awoke in a hot sweat. I had seen a cat's head floating about in the darkness. I looked up 'cat' in the dream book and it said that cats in dreams are a symbol for your intuition, and that the health of the cat indicated whether you were heeding or ignoring your intuition. I knew I had to get closer to Saturn Return. I knew I needed to escape.

Neon Illuminations

If you have a friend,

treat her as such,

never let that friend learn too much,

for if that friend becomes your foe,

around the world your secrets go

(Nan 1979)

21A window seat with a view of the cotton wool clouds. Transcending the skies, I left behind the mayhem of burglary-gate. Boarding the Boeing 747 I felt safe in the knowledge that escaping would liberate me in my search for purpose, and with less than six weeks to the big three zero I was finally beginning to feel like I was making progress. Perhaps Saturn was now looking at me in a new light. I felt like perhaps it was possible.

No matter how blinded you are to change,

no journey is devoid of an internal gearshift, with the departure lounge at an airport providing the right sanctuary for this to start. It's a place where you can fuse two worlds together. Either the unknown with the familiar, or of two worlds colliding. I was returning to a place I had once called home; a transient city where everyone was consumed with leaving, where everyone talked about escaping. I was finally on my way to Hong Kong.

As the plane glided through the blistering sunset into the dead of night, the orange glow dissolved as the aircraft drew Etch A Sketch markings in the sky. It was hard to believe this was really happening. I knew arriving would lack some of the excitement of the old Kai Tak airport where descending onto Kowloon Bay it was like flying into a glamorous movie set with its breathtaking views of the metropolis almost clipping the city's densely packed apartment buildings and neon-lit skyscrapers. The plane came to a stop on the runway, which was surrounded by water.

Waiting nervously for Rita at the newer Chek Lap Kok airport the taste of Tsing Toa beer greeted me with the comfort of an old friend. Perched on the chrome and plastic red barstool it felt as if I hadn't been away and my life in London was all a mere illusion. The sense of familiarity was surprisingly reassuring; the level of noise had intensified, smells hung in the air like an overbearing perfume, and the humidity was as hard hitting as if entering a sauna.

When I had returned from Manila in 1989, after being treated for a rampant amoeba - a nasty stomach condition that attacks your intestines - Rita had spent a year in India travelling. She had returned like so many others to Hong Kong on her way back to Europe and decided to stay on. We had kept in touch sporadically; sending letters across the continents over the years. This was, pre-social media when letter writing had more of a craft about it. From both sides there was an aversion to calling on the phone - partially to keep the friendship in a time and place where it was founded. This was in an era pre-mass telecommunications where long haul travel made relationships long distance, and where these long-lasting relationships could stop and start from where you left them.

Rita arrived late, not as I had initially thought because she had been gridlocked in the dense and heavily polluted traffic that raged through the city twenty-four/seven. Looking pale and gaunt but with the same wiry mass of hair and still dressed in black cottons she hugged me as if her life depended on it. With my encouragement she drank, albeit at the speed of inhalation, enough alcohol to bring some colour into her cheeks. It was after her third bottle of beer she pushed forward a large leather holdall that had been sitting beside her like an obedient Labrador.

It transpired the bag contained her life belongings. She had, moments before, walked out on Henry her long-term partner and traded him in for an up and coming martial arts stunt man; Roddy Lau. I was not being whisked off to Henry's lavish apartment in the Peak as anticipated, which at 1,811 feet above sea level, was the highest point on Hong Kong Island and towered above the heart of the city with spectacular three hundred and sixty-degree panoramic views of the surrounding islands, and where I had hoped to shake off my jet lag and relax in luxury. Instead, we bundled ourselves into a green taxi and headed for a small village in the New Territories, where Roddy had a holiday home.

After being suspended in the air for over thirteen hours and travelling for almost twenty, the bottle of brandy kept for special occasions in Roddy's flat was the perfect cure to ease an aching body, and after toasting 'new beginnings' it provided a good excuse to go to bed early and leave the newly declared relationship to itself.

I didn't mind having to share the box room with a wooden man, a walnut coloured totem pole which bore branches out of it (good for hanging clothes by the way,) it was the racket of Mahjong that banged through my head like a defected MPEG mixed with the barking dogs, varying pitches of voices in the background, Canto pop, karaoke and crickets.

I spent the first part of the night trying to

track a gecko that was hanging to the ceiling directly above my head. The first time I had seen one of these magical lizards, I had thought it was a baby crocodile but later learnt these make for good houseguests as they eat all the unwanted insects, and are deemed as lucky. Whether it was because staring at one object can help meditation or whether the alcohol had taken effect, I no longer wanted to worry about the wildlife sharing the room with me and I found myself lost in the world of sleep. Only to wake abruptly to find myself double the size I was before leaving London. Hands, face, legs, feet all swollen to grotesque proportions.

Rica had let herself in and was busy cleaning the kitchen when I awoke. We took coffee together and she told me her life story. Rica was a gentle soul. She told me she had four children who were all living in the

Philippines with her husband and that she had not been working before coming to Hong Kong as a domestic worker. She was saving for her children's education and was happy to be working for several clients. We talked in hushed whispers and crept about like mime artists so as not to wake Rita and Roddy, until it got so late the balance tipped and it felt as if they should be checked on. Pushing open the bedroom door, the mirrored wardrobe provided a three sixty view of an empty room. They had gone. No SMS, no note, no message, nothing. I tried Rita's mobile. It was switched off. The disappointment was like a static shock. Rita and I were kindred spirits - soul sisters. Our friendship was unconditional. We had spent years expressing letters back and forth across the oceans underlying the longing to see one another. Just like the old days she was going to put the world to rights, but she was nowhere to be seen.

The room smelt of humidity and stale sex. A Formica dressing table, covered in toothpicks and scratch cards overlaid with Rita's jewelry accessories, stood in front of the window. I opened the blind. Downstairs on the crazy paved garden a pair of old women were gracefully doing tai chi. How different they were to my Nan - I could never have persuaded her to go out and glide. Turning back to the main room there was for the first time a silence; the silence you feel when the rest of the world is turning, and you realise you are alone with nothing to do.

Waiting for the green and pastel yellow mini-bus the heat outside was overwhelming. Apart from an old man taking his Songbirds for a walk there were no other passengers. It reminded me of the pair of Lovebirds we had as children, in our small garden farm. Since they are not solitary birds by nature and prefer the company of their own kind these friendly, inquisitive, colourful, and intelligent birds lived together until one of them fell sick. My Dad put the ailing bird in a shoebox with a lamp over its body like a halo providing heat and tried unsuccessfully to nurse it back to life by hand feeding him. His mate seemed so lost to be left behind, hanging around like a Walasse Ting print at the back of the aviary that within hours of his passing, his mate died too.

The bus stopped directly in front of a market that masked the entrance to the Metro. A patchwork of red and white-striped awnings decoratively displayed meat from steel hooks with spotlight bulbs brightening the red blood-stained carcasses. Poultry in wicker baskets lined the underbelly of the wooden butcher tables. From red plastic buckets hung offal. Side-stepping past a floor saturated in water and feathers I headed down into the underground.

The air-conditioned stainless-steel carriage provided a refreshing contrast to the naked skin from the heat outdoors. Going from the New Territories to Hong Kong Island I tried not to crash into my neighbour's lap. As if in a poorly attempted ski plough, it was difficult not to knock people flying as the train curved and sped through the tunnels. An orange clad Hare Krishna got on at Mong Kok and sat next to me. Anyone who has ever worked in Soho square will have 'that' chant circling around in their head every time they see a Hare Krishna as they secretly wish they would come and rescue them from the mundane routine of work life.

Exiting the Metro in Central where evolving building developments were spreading like wild fire, I marvelled at the changing face of this city. Ignoring the desire, like many, to leap into the emporium of global fashion brands, I headed towards to the Mandarin Hotel to use the facilities. The bathroom, a white marbled room covered in a white carpet of serious shag pile, eased the pressure off hot blistered feet. Staring down at my burning soles for a fleeting moment, I massaged them into the weave and contemplated learning the art of reflexology. If your feet are the navigation map to the rest of your body, it's best to take good care of them. The walls were embossed with gold leaf off-set by grand baby blue satin curtains framing the drop windows. An ornate glass dressing table full of designer perfumes, enough to open a small perfumery, were all available for you to try. On standby was a toilet attendant ready to brush imaginary hairs from your shoulders when you had finished checking yourself in the larger than life mirror, whilst in the distance, a string quartet could be heard entertaining the afternoon tea guests. This was probably one of the best toilets in the world.

There were two rates for the boat that ferries people to Lantau Island situated at the mouth of the Pearl River, one pumped up and one very cheap. One entitled the passenger to sit outside on the top deck where you could catch third degrees burns watching the boat trawl through an oil bed of pollution, or, you could squash together in the belly of the ship in air-conditioned comfort listening to the roar of the engine and inhale oil fumes. Of the choices there was nothing more exhilarating than watching the city's skyscrapers disappear behind you as you headed out into the vastness of the South China Sea. On this occasion it felt like the right thing to do - a good moment in time to remember Rafe.

The harbour was always littered with

bustling junks, ferries and san pans. The boat people were known as the 'egg' people as traditionally they paid their taxes in the currency of eggs, and it was not uncommon for them to live, marry and die without ever leaving the water, even though the government was encouraging them to come ashore so that their children could go to school. These were proper water babies.

Transferring from wet to dry land I took a bus at Mui Wo up towards the monastery. The lush greenery and distant paddy fields took the ache out of travelling. The simplicity of nature's environment can be so seductively alluring; this was what it is all about... surely? I could live like this, working in the paddy fields by day, gathering fresh food, being at one with nature and living with just the essentials. It all seemed very appealing. Perhaps this was the way to make Saturn

Return and to become a completed person, aged thirty?

The bus halted as we reached mid-point on the steep hill. Several passengers prepared to disembark, when I was suddenly shoved forward, so that without choice, I was compelled to dive into the lunge position. Two gold-capped teeth hawkers shouted to each other inches apart from one another. Both dressed in generic uniforms of black baggy trousers and patterned shirts with straw hats hanging loosely down their backs. They did vocal battle with one another occasionally gesticulating towards me. The driver retorted sending the two women retreating from the bus dragging me with them.

My overpriced, once in a life time designer rucksack, had managed to get attached to one of the hawker's baskets with my hand still clasped in the handle, in the commotion and a small child came to my rescue. His mother attempted to grab her son out of the scene and the doors closed just as one of hawkers ground her teeth and spat - aiming at the ground where I had put the bag down to release the child. As we continued our uphill climb I wiped the remaining phlegm off my much-loved accessory, thinking how tough it would be to live out here in the wilderness.

Taking the Wisdom Path trail up to Tian Tan Buddha I arrived where thirty-eight timber columns carved a mountainous masterpiece of the Heart Sutra written in calligraphy. Craning my neck, I focused ahead at the ascending climb. In the same agony as exercising on the power plate I struggled to the top. The Buddha's rotund stomach protruded outwards masking the view until the last steps where the reward was a bird's eye view of the island, a humbling experience as you recognised your own insignificance high up against this monumental bronzed statue. The heat seemed to be a deterrent from tourist crowds so in solitary I sat and pondered.

Was the answer embedded in Buddha like a pearl inside an oyster? Could I puzzle out Saturn Return? Climbing to the furthest possible peak I soaked in the panoramic view and inhaled the fresh air. This had been an exhausting forty-eight hours. Searching for a place to rest, I managed to nestle into the swell of Tian Tan's lotus position, the crotch of Buddha. All I really needed now was some rest. I lay down and closed my eyes.

A mass of grey cloth approached me, shouting and beckoned me down from the Buddha. The brilliant light of the day's sky now blackened by dark rain clouds - supported by a wind whipping up a storm from the heavens. The man, who didn't seem very meditative at all, was trying to usher me out of the empty monastery with rapid speed. In a semi sleep I marched back down the two hundred and sixty-eight steps, and before I had time to recover I was outside the closed gates, sunburnt and dehydrated.

I had intended to visit the glittering night market, dazzling with traditional spirit, where remnants of ancient China flourished, in the hope to see a Chinese opera. Nightlife on the streets in Hong Kong never failed to impress but the impending downpour erupted, and the typhoon signal was released. It was enough of an effort to make it back to the love shack in the New Territories before the weather became too ferocious to be outdoors.

****

Rita said they had gone shopping and we must have missed each other as our paths crossed.

That was on the first day. After that she didn't bother to invent any excuses. She took to enjoying an illicit time with Roddy, from bed to bathroom, from sunrise to sunset. When I finally approached the subject, she told me in no uncertain terms that Roddy was her life now and that he came first. Every time I tried to leverage this by reminding her of our shared nostalgia, my pleas were ignored. Rita explained that she had spent a long time looking for happiness and now she had found it, she would do everything that was necessary to keep it, and silenced any conversation by repeatedly playing Des'ree *I Ain't Movin'* on full volume.

I rang Lulu to explain I was returning to England earlier than planned and wouldn't be able to meet up. Lulu had been a friend of Rafe and Monique; we had met at one of the night parties in Causeway Bay. Before I had finished our conversation, Lulu had ordered a taxi, insisting that I move out and stay with her for a few days.

Lulu, an elfin woman with punky blonde hair lived in the Hollywood Road; the antique district, just above the heart of the Central. By contrast, her flat provided a peaceful sanctuary with its high ceilings and large windows creating light and air different to that of the partitioned walls and low roofing of Roddy's steamy flat. A magnificent hand carved bookshelf from Nepal ran down one side of the room, with a pair of steel treasure chests on the other side. Korean wall hangings fell from picture rails to the floor, which was covered by Japanese Fendi rugs. Silk cushions were scattered over a French chaise longue. A large ceiling fan and a snake plant breathed life into the living room, which was beautifully decorated with antique curios found from the surrounding streets. The tower block windows drew in a view of some of more of the famous sky scrapers that soared the skyline; including the momentous Hong Kong bank with its design resembling the back of a fridge - each marking a memory from the distant past.

We talked about the years apart, how much we had grown as people, and yet, how the much the same we really were. Lulu had herself married and divorced and was running a small art gallery where she exhibited the work of several artists she managed and that brought her the satisfaction she was looking for. After all, she had stayed in China post 1997, had made her future and was happy to call this place her home.

With absolute ease I told her about Saturn Return and why I had come on such a journey. Lulu told me one of her artists Candice, was doing an installation video art piece on fertility in the gallery and that since Saturn Return is about rebirth and new beginnings she recommended I should get involved. She said she felt that my visit had synchronicity with the timing of the project and I thought this could be a sign. She also said I could stay at her place for as long as I wanted and take time to have a proper holiday, visiting old haunts. I didn't really want to get involved with the art thing but couldn't see a polite way out of it given I was receiving such wonderful hospitality. So, I agreed to meet Taylor the project leader... erm, I mean, the director.

Taylor, told us that we were to find our hidden potential to develop our natural talents, and that would raise our inner confidence. We were needed for three rehearsal sessions and on the third she would film us. On the first session I spent two hours on my back ticking like a clock. Taylor said I would be representing the biological calling of nature and would be providing the rhythm for the rest of the group. Rather like a metronome I was there to literally set the pace.

Afterwards we all went to the Fringe Club in Lan Kwai Fong for drinks. I felt compromised as I really needed to spend time on my Saturn Return, so I told Taylor that I was sorry, and it wasn't for me. Rather seasoned in push back she was having none of it, and told me I was suffering from mild performance pressure and that she wasn't looking for results, she just wanted people to have a go and release their inner inhibition.

There may have been some truth in her analysis of the situation. The last time I had been involved in anything remotely theatrical was when I had selected to crown the statue of Our Lady, on May Day 1980. It was a strange turn of events, as year on year the prettiest girl in the class was called forward to be Mary - a totally biased selection process. Eventually after a parent pressure group arose, the decision was made to put all the girls' names on raffle tickets folded up into a tambourine for the headmistress to select someone randomly. I vividly remember watching Sister Jaleh's claw like hand fumble about with the tiny squares of faded pink paper searching, and I'm sure praying, she was picking the right girl. As she plucked the winning ticket from the instrument and viewed the results, I saw the dismay in her eyes. What I didn't expect was to hear my name being called out. In that moment, I knew I was doomed to fail. After all, I was no Mary.

The rehearsal however, did seem to go well, but on the actual day I was besieged by fear and standing alone at the alter in a long white virgin dress I recall looking up at the crucifix and seeing Dick Turpin riding toward me on a huge black horse. The horse reared inches from my feet causing the masked highway man to pull a pistol and shoot me in the head.

It seems I had blacked out and fainted, and Dick was part of a dream. They said it could have been the thurible that had intoxicated me. A very tall pubescent altar boy carried me out of the church on to the Covent lawns, where I had been moments before on a pair of step ladders covered in daisy chains placing a cardboard golden frame around a life size model of the Mother Mary. It had been such a public display of shame and humiliation, from there on in I tried to channel my disappointment into sticking to all activities behind the scenes.

I put my hand on Taylor and pressing firmly, told her in the deepest voice I could muster, that I was okay in not taking part in the project, and only then she backed down, asking if I wanted to represent Aphrodite instead, but I said I didn't want to represent anything, apart from myself. So, there we left it, at the bar in the Fringe Club, and the project was never mentioned again.

Lulu suggested I saw her herbalist as she thought I could be suffering from stress. The aches in my stomach were becoming too frequent to be ignored. Lulu said there was good and bad stress and I was somewhere in between. She told me that good stress could be triggered by something that heightened your sense of emotion, like a film or sport - something that sets your adrenaline pumping. Bad stress was more often centred around negative emotions and unhelpful thinking which made sense of my relationships and career anxiety. I was happy to have a balanced diagnostic for once until she explained it was the bad stress that was the worst kind to bring on viral infections and immune deficiencies. Great. I had felt sluggish since the bike accident and knew that I had been living off a reserve of fitness left over from when I was active with swimming and kickboxing. This reserve was now running low, it was true. I hadn't been near jogging bottoms or trainers for too long to remember, and as a result my body had manifested itself into an ensemble of tiredness. I wondered if this was a direct link from the rampant amoeba I had caught years ago, or if there was something else lurking inside. To avoid suffering in ignorance, I took her advice and hit the herbalists.

The prescription they concocted for me was a brew of phosphorus and yam. A Chinese calligraphy report sheet translated that I had poly problems so there was much hope attached to this herbal medicine to start the curing process. More than one problem, all parts of the body malfunctioning, teeth aching, unable to hear, unable to see clearly, it's an effort to hold yourself up sometimes.

The huge airy shop smelt of musky wood emitting from bulbous glass jars, shaped like demijohns, containing like a box of chocolates - a myriad of tastes. Remedies of tree bark, and reindeer penis, exposed in jars with the most bizarre collection of fossilized life. Minute ornate wooden boxes housed smaller, leafier herbs and potions, each meticulously measured out on old-fashioned wrought iron scales. Purchasing herbs was far from a hurried affair, things were taken slowly and methodically, as the white coated specialists weighed up the exact proportions, customers were invited to sit front of house and sip on green tea whilst observing the line drawing poster of the human body pin pointing the meridians healed by acupuncture.

After a while I got used to the rise and swell of the stomach and resigned myself that it had a life of its own and that I would never be one of those fortunate women who had it flat. Its acceptance isn't it, that you're not a teenager any more, and at its best you can use the bulge to look maternal, which for some people can be a turn on. It develops its own personality too, especially when you are dating. It becomes a case of,

'Hello, this is me. Now let me introduce you to my stomach'.

Dexter had once accompanied me to St. Thomas A&E on a Friday night because my stomach had extended so far, I looked six months pregnant. The wait time was so long, we ended up ordering in pizza whilst he sang to everyone in outpatients before taking a cab home because we couldn't be bothered to queue any longer.

The word 'poly' was a concern for me. Was there something more sinister inside me? What if I was infertile? Not that I wanted kids right now but the idea of having it taken away from me... Especially as nobody tells you anything until it is too late. What is it about when you reach twenty-nine and you are already threading, waxing, plucking and shaving? Not only is there a moustache to contend with but also the beard sets in. You could be in the middle of a high-class flirt when unwittingly you catch a glimpse of yourself, and the only thing that stands out is a rebel hair poking itself way out of your chin. Your back gets fatter. Your biceps vanish, making it look like you have no sculptured lines to your body at all. Your legs begin to show vein tracks – even the neck shows signs of sagging skin as everything is besieged by gravity and moves downwards.

Later, Doctor Annie Wong at Tsan Yuk Hospital showed me the scan and confirmed that there was nothing wrong apart from constipation and no direct link to the rampant amoeba caught in the Philippines. She said I should eat little and often, which is the same advice Nan always gave; a hangover from the 1940s, and she gave me a nutrition sheet. She suggested there were several problems to do with digestion but that these should improve by regularly drinking water and sticking to an improved, nutritious diet. No more fad diets.

Dr. Wong said at best I should take responsibility for my health and at worst eating the wrong foods or forgetting to eat would undo all the good work. Forgetting to eat? There has always been a mystery to me about those people who claim they 'forget' to eat. You can forget to pay a bill, the water rates or your television licence, but eat? I guess the fruit and wine diet hadn't really paid off. So, it was good news that I would be entering the new dawn of adulthood with the possibility of a fit body and mind and now I had the wherewithal to do it.

The ex–Causeway Bay crowd, those few who remained, threw a party on the eve of my departure. There were very few people left in Hong Kong from the past. Most had migrated elsewhere around the world. For those who had stayed or returned, and many did return periodically, it was like being with family again. There is something about the intensity of friendships built outside of your homeland. Meeting outside of the confines of your family, away from your comfort zone, can bring a unique quality to the partnership;

making it in many ways more romantic and with a sense of deep connection. A collective of kindred spirits.

I thought about inviting Rita, but some things were best left undone. I had so very much wanted to relive the closeness we had once shared and for everything to be the same as it had been, but what had happened between us was less of a result of what we had together, and more about who we really were. Our priorities were different now, and where I had been living in the past, she had moved on and out into her future. Ten years ago, she was in her Saturn Return and in some ways, I had expected her to still be there. How curious that I had thought her to be so messed up yet still so very in control of things. How funny is it that youth can let you believe you would do things differently, be different, that you have all the time in the world to get things right, when in fact there is no head start on how things are going to turn out.

The party moved between the live music venues Dusk to Dawn and The Wanch, where we danced late into the night. Only breaking away at internals to take a reprieve outside, propping our body weight up against the corrugated steel shutters of the shop fronts, and smoked menthol cigarettes, whilst proclaiming that we didn't smoke at all.

With an early flight this was the best way to exit the city. Taylor came along with the fertility group and we made quite a collective of party revellers. Amidst the bump and grind there were some deliriously happy people. What an absolute joy to watch people having so much fun, and how fabulous everyone looked - so carefree.

The last I saw of Lulu was singing a bad rendition of 'Still Haven't Found What I'm

Looking For' in the back streets of Wan Chai. The tequila was out in force and there were signs things were getting seriously messy. My feet were beginning to trip me up, so I slipped out the door when no one was looking. No goodbyes.

Outside, the street life was as wired with its neon energy as it was inside the dark confines of the glitter ball club. Through a haze of alcohol, the bright candy coloured lights soared like shooting stars, and the late-night shops and bars lined the pavements with activity to the sound of the ever-present noise of the clacking pedestrian signals.

To the right, lay the waterfront, with ships of varying sizes disappearing in and out of the harbour. The smaller ones bobbed about like plastic toys in a bath. On the left were the dragon hills, where concrete met cloud in a Feng shui union. Amidst the noise and chaos was nature and tranquility. In this heady night light, I realised that there is no real place that you can call home. It's not location, or real estate, or fabric and materials. Home is a place you create in the mind; a safe place which you can return when you need to escape all the clutter and noise of everyday life.

The journey to the airport was seamless as the roads took a reprieve before the day's exhausting traffic started up. From the red taxi window, I could see the shift of day between folk returning home and the early risers. The airport, equally empty, created a sobering atmosphere. As the passengers filed their way down the aisle I looked behind at the long trail and started to make a wish that the seat next to me would be free from screaming babies, anyone who was too talkative, had air sickness, or smelt.

Knowing there would be a wait time as the

plane taxied out of the airport, I got into position; seat back, blanket on lap, pillow at the window. Ah and, relax. A young boy came over joined by an air stewardess who asked if I minded if he sat next to me. I mustered a jokey tone saying that it was okay as long as he sat still and let me sleep. The boy laughed and said,

'We'll see!'

Like, what now?

A kid with attitude. Why me?

What I really meant was so long as you leave me alone.

By the time we had reached the Middle East, Louie was my mate. He told me he had been in a long-term relationship and now needed space. That his last girlfriend had run off with his best friend, who, in a cruel twist of fate had dumped her after one date. I told him

I thought he was too young to be snarled up in long-term relationships and he reminded me that kids of his age had kids of their own. He didn't eat much; a boiled egg minus the yolk, water and orange juice. He said plane food was not particularly good for anyone and that it was unattractive to let yourself go, then without any encouragement he lifted his American Apparel sweat shirt and showed me his six pack. I tried to educate him on the perils of not eating enough, but he did not succumb to my sales patter. He said he liked singing and would try for a reality show, then he busted out a song with real tears in his eyes at the sad bits. I had to admit, he had a nice tone and we chatted all the way home.

It wasn't until we were flying past France and entering the white cliffs of Dover into the UK that when checking my face in the toilet mirror it dawned on me. The trip had been enlightening and with only three weeks to go until my thirtieth birthday I wasn't as scared as I thought I would be. I would continue to focus on Saturn Return and be less worried about things, I would look after my body and mind, and I would slow down. It was then I understood something terrible about myself. Looking at my reflection in the tiny aircraft bathroom, I realised I had been flirting with a seventeen-year-old, with no makeup on.

It wasn't just because the man jumping up and down was flailing his arms around absurdly; it was because he was pale skinned, semi naked, wearing only a pair of beige knee length shorts with fluffy white ankle socks and sandals that I found it most distracting. I picked up speed, trying to edge past all the weary travellers searching for their friends and families as they walked down the aisle, where the crowds were gathering at the arrivals gate.

It wasn't until I got closer to the end of the walkway I recognised that the man was my Dad. As I approached, I saw he was inviting the crowd to look at his scars, which ran from his chest down both sides of his legs. In the style of a street statue minus the blue silver body paint, he stood with his arms out in the arrested position slowly twirling around to show the lines on his body to his private audience, with the same pride as if they were military medals awarded for bravery.

In a loud stage whisper Mum, who was among the ensemble of spectators, explained that whilst he looked the same, it would be a while before Dad would be back to his old self. His behaviour was part of coming to terms with the magnitude of his open-heart surgery, and until he was ready, we would just have to support his waves of exhibitionism.

I hadn't expected them to be at the airport, so it came as a surprise as I was led into an all-day breakfast restaurant where my parents like bookends sandwiched me in between them. Most of the tables were spilling over with families and their luggage so we moved towards the back of the café where they chose a cluster of hard back chairs.

'Dad's cleared out the aviary and he's made it into a lovely den...'

'A den?' I queried.

'Yes. Like, what's the word?... Pog, Po-god? Your friend has one in the garden? They are very useful, you know, you slept in it. Oh, what's it called?'

'Pagoda? Sam has a pagoda.'

'All your things you left behind are in there now. It looks good.' Mum smiled.

'Why?'

My parents shared a look – the kind of look between their eyes that transmuted a multitude of possibilities, each pausing for the other to speak, until Mum couldn't contain herself any longer.

'Zoe, there is plenty of space'

'Why are my things in there and not in the loft?' I demanded.

'You've been burgled… You're not happy in Balham… It's expensive… We think you should go and live with Nan'

'I am happy there'

'Your Mother said when she stayed with you it was very noisy, and you've got no real living space, so why don't you live with her until you are on your feet again?' Dad intervened.

'I'm nearly thirty, I can't live my Nan!' I stared at them.

'Why ever not?'

'For a start, she doesn't live in London...'

'Well, we don't see a way around it, unless you put more effort into getting regular work how are you going to manage?'

'But I do have regular work...'

'This past year you've not been yourself, and we appreciate we've all had a lot on, but it can't go on like this. At some point you are going to have to make some decisions about what you want in life. We're not saying move there forever, it's just a stop gap, but we have been very worried about you and it's not good for your health to be living like that.'

'Like what?' I was incredulous.

'Mum's right,' Dad said. 'We'll support whatever you want to do in life, you know that, so long as you're happy. Right now, you need a focus and you need to earn some cash.

Life is for living Zoe, and time passes by very quickly. You've only got a short time on this planet and you have to grab things whilst you still can.'

'I do make a living.'

'We're not expecting you to give us an answer right now, but think about it, overnight?'

A dark haired, round faced, incredibly cute looking Spanish-speaking toddler with piercing aqua blue eyes, decided to abandon her family a few tables away and came to sit next to me. She picked out bits of muffin from where it had been embedded into the upholstery of the chair and made a small pile of sponge on the coffee table that separated her and my parents. Mum signalled at her family not too far behind as Dad winked at the little girl; giving her permission to stay with us.

'There is something I should tell you…'

A group of students caused a diversion as they entered in fancy dress with buckets of coins they shook like rattles as they pitched for cash for charity. The place was highly animated, and everyone got caught up in the merriment. The little girl's eyes were burning into me, so I poked my tongue out sideways as a playful gesture to her. The students moved towards us and hovered behind my Dad's back and plastered a sticky label onto his chest with a slogan raising support for their campaign. Mum fumbled around for loose change as a way of releasing him from the pressure. My parents looked at me quizzically; Mother's glare on my stomach, while Dad looked in a feigned nonchalant way straight on. The little girl now poked her tongue out to the side whilst turning her head until she was looking at me with her smiley moon face upside down.

'I am in my Saturn Return. It's a phase

when everything changes' I explained.

'What sort of change? What do you mean?'

'Everything. I am questioning everything right now and trying to find out who I really am.'

'Nothing to do with drugs, is it?'

'Mum! Look – Saturn - a part of me that I've neglected and want to win back

'Is it that chap? Is he bothering you? The one you were dating who left you to look after his ex-girlfriend's cat?'

'No.'

'Look we can only go on what you tell us, and you said...'

'No, nothing like that. Look, there is an astrological belief that every twenty-nine years, the planets are aligned in the same position as when you were born, and this means each person will go through major change and upheaval in their twenty-ninth year and it's a time, like a rebirth, to start again.'

The little girl now lay flat out on the table, bored with our conversation, trying to cover herself in newspapers that had been left scattered on the floor.

'But you need to be focusing on what you want out of life, not expecting things to happen all the time. There are no miracles' Mum went on.

'You're missing the point, I am discovering what I will do by waiting for my Saturn Return. Everyone goes through it. You did!'

'We didn't have this type of thing when we were your age, we just had to get on with it' Mum sighed.

'You went through major change when you were twenty-nine! You moved from the Middle East to Europe, Grandad died, Dad changed his profession… There is lots of proof - you both went through upheaval and change'

'What we are saying is, that if you want to "win" as you say, get your Saturn back, or however you want to call it, you need to do something about it and you won't do that sitting in a bedsit in Balham.'

'I know that, and that's what I've been doing! I've been taking courses and having some treatments to better understand what is going on…' I explained.

'Unpaid.'

'What?'

'You don't get paid for that?'

'No, I don't get paid for that… In the same way you don't get paid for just existing… but I am working on the side - I am freelancing.'

An uncomfortable silence left us mute. The little girl used this as a cue to rise, offering my

Dad a sheet of newspaper before she stepped off the table and returned to her original seat.

'So long as you are doing something about the future, then you'll be alright then, won't you?'

'Yes' I said. 'Yes, I will.'

Sweet Blue Something

I must go down to the sea again,

the lonely shore and the sky,

I left my vest and pants there,

I wonder if they are dry

(Nan 1980)

The things you worry about are often solved in a way you could not ever have imagined happening. Dexter was so happy to see me return safely from Asia. He told me the news that our landlord Terry had decided to sell the house and that everyone had been given formal notice. We had a month to leave, which would coincide with the dreaded thirtieth. There was, however, a greater sweetness to this news. As the longest serving tenants, we would both be awarded with one thousand pounds compensation. Dexter had already put a deposit on a one bed in Tooting. He needed the space. His work was flourishing, and he was becoming prolific in his own right with his musical talents. He had also met someone whom he was serious about and was really hoping to make it all work.

We decided against a leaving party, as we wanted to ensure our compensation bond was not jeopardised, and since we had both been invited to an opening of an art gallery in Shoreditch we decided this would be our big final night together before we moved out, for good.

The exhibition heralded the emerging talent of Mexican artists; exhibiting brilliant assemblage art on the theme of the Day of the Dead. These pieces encapsulated people's ancestry and were so clever and so awe inspiring I wondered how long it would take before I could become an artist. Not that I'd ever wanted to be one, it just suddenly became an appealing idea.

After the preview, the gallery transformed into a performance space; with poets waxing lyrical, singer-songwriters, and a video installation piece running on loop without any sound. Big, bright images projected onto the floors and ceiling. Before the close of the night, the compere invited people up to the podium to do shout outs, which were rather like calls to action. These ranged from individuals giving praise to one another, to a guy named Pete from Peckham who said he was looking for volunteers to help with a local homelessness charity. Eric asked if anyone wanted to be an extra for a short film he was making about the rise of local breweries, and Pratima was looking for some paid admin support for a food festival in Shropshire. Then Julian stood up and said he was looking for new tenants for his house in Finsbury Park. I raised my hand before anyone else could, feeling rather pleased as if I had just won a bid at the contemporary art exhibition at Christie's auction house. After the shout outs had finished, the studio closed, and we were invited back to a local house to continue into the night. The last time I saw Dexter he was captivating an audience by doing the caterpillar across the kitchen floor. In that moment, I knew this had been a time that I would cherish. I was beginning to feel excited about the future with all its endless possibilities, and I felt safe in the belief that real friendship, finds its way back to you.

I arranged to meet Julian early the next week to view the accommodation, but he had to go away on business, and instead I was greeted by his parents, who were visiting from China. I thought this must be a sign. They didn't say much but showed me around the vast space. The basement entrance was through a hatch in the kitchen and was completely fitted out in a nautical style with parquet flooring. It was the den of the house and had great stereo equipment integrated into the walls. The lounge had a 1950s vintage retro bar with furniture to match, and up on the first floor, the master bedroom came with a Juliet balcony overlooking what had been the garage and had been converted into a rose garden courtyard. The place was spacious - a complete contrast to the shabby bedsit in Balham. There were artefacts from Asia scattered around, and this felt like the right place to be.

It turned out that Julian, an environmental lawyer, wanted more than just a tenant. He needed someone to find other tenants for the three-bed house and oversee the property. He was due to start a secondment in Beijing and didn't want to hand the responsibility over to the care of any estate agent. This additional work came with the perks of a reduced rent, and first dibs on the bedrooms. I agreed immediately to these conditions, dyed my hair aubergine, bought a push bike, and left the flat lay lines of South London to head up North.

Julian, however, had already promised the same deal to a young Hungarian girl named Sofia. Sofia didn't care for the additional responsibilities so quickly opted for the smaller bedroom and let me handle the rest of it. At the same time, I offered the basement out to Mark; a fellow freelance work colleague who was on a three-month management training course. Then Isabella, the Mexican artist from the gallery turned up, saying she needed space from her husband. Mark moved onto the sofa and Isabella took the basement. Except Isabella's husband missed her so much, he visited every day and stayed over most nights. Then Kimberly arrived. I hadn't seen her since the wedding, and she needed somewhere to crash two nights a week, as her job brought her to the city for meetings. This was not the kind of tenant management I had imagined, but it was the summer and it was hot, and I was nearly thirty.

Next door lived an artist named Elliot who visited often; there was a conjoined pathway from the courtyard into his studio. We hung out together and after a while he asked if I'd be his business manager. It seemed in less than a month, I had a new home, new friends, and a new job.

Everything seemed fine until the eve of my thirtieth, when I read a headline in a feature article about stress inducing events, and discovered moving was in the top three. I could feel my breathing become shallower, a headache thumped the sides of my forehead, and I felt nauseous. Death was in the top three, as well as divorce. It said nothing about turning thirty. I tried my relaxing techniques, but nothing seemed to work. The scented bath burnt my skin and the oils caught in the back of my throat and made me choke. I took a short walk but there was an undercurrent of tension on the streets, and alcohol miniatures littered the pavements. These little bottles were discarded make shift crack pipes.

Listening to relaxing music made me angry, and I was too stressed to read about mindfulness. I couldn't find a way out of escaping how I was feeling and it was making me jumpy. Everyone was out, and the house creaked in the silence. I tried to sleep by squashing my head between pillows to shut everything out. When this didn't work, I decided to write down exactly what I was thinking, so I could see what was really bothering me, and if it was worth the worry. In doing so I discovered some things which I had recently learnt.

Unhappiness is fleeting. It's like a passing cloud and it is better to seek meaning without focusing on whether you are happy in that moment. Having meaningful relationships helps you feel connected. Where would we be without the friends we meet along the way? Finding purpose in what you are doing makes you feel good about yourself. You don't have to love your job to find purpose in your life, and having a goal changes the way you see the world. The only way to beat procrastination, is to get started. Self-care is important too: sleeping well, eating nutritious foods and exercise all contribute to feeling good.

I notice that I feel much better having put this down on the page to reflect on these revelations.

It's midnight. In less than ten minutes I will be entering a new decade. I look out over the balcony at beautiful roses which are silhouetted by the darkness of night, and which gently sway in the soft warm summer breeze. The crescent moon shines down, as I listen to the sound of urban life in the residential street below, and let out a sigh. What would I tell my ten-year-old self? I ponder, and I realise I would tell her, that 'Everything is going to be ok'. I look at my phone, it's eight minutes past midnight. Then it dawns on me, I have witnessed my Saturn Return, and I'm home.

About the Author

Angie writes for digital portals about personal performance and has authored the book, *52 Little Tips on Big Ways to Improve Your Wellbeing.*

Angie has also written *Diving for Pearls*, a stage play set at the Tooting Bec Lido, South London, that premiered at the Albany Theatre in Deptford; and wrote and performed *Eve*, a one-person play, at the Tristan Bates Theatre, London. She spent two years as a theatre reviewer for What's *on in London*.

Last Exit to Balham is Angie's first novella.

Printed in Great Britain
by Amazon